W9-BSC-848

WHEN NOBODY ELSE WILL DO IT . . .
WHEN NOBODY ELSE CAN DO IT . . .
CALL IN THE A-TEAM

When a hot-shot reporter tracks down a story in Mexico that threatens to put his byline on a tombstone, it's time to call . . .

THE A-TEAM

When a Mexican village is overrun by a small army of bandidos and a vicious killer sets himself up as law, it's time to call . . .

THE A-TEAM

And when a beautiful young journalist, searching for her missing colleague, hires Hannibal Smith, B. A. Baracus, Face Man, and Howling Mad Murdock, she's got herself more than a handful of high jinks. They're the smartest, meanest, toughest, craziest bunch of vets who ever tackled trouble. That's why they're called . . .

THE A-TEAM

THE A-TEAM

Novel by
Charles Heath
Based on the television series *A-TEAM*
Created by Frank Lupo & Stephen J. Cannell
Adapted from the pilot episode *A-TEAM*
Written by
Frank Lupo & Stephen J. Cannell

A DELL BOOK

Published by
Dell Publishing Co., Inc.
1 Dag Hammarskjold Plaza
New York, New York 10017

A-TEAM is a trademark of Stephen J. Cannell Productions
and licensed by Universal City Studios, Inc.

Dell ® TM 681510, Dell Publishing Co., Inc.

ISBN: 0-440-10009-7

Printed in the United States of America
First printing—January 1984

PROLOGUE

The large bell in the old church tower pealed mournfully as a hot wind rolled through the elevated streets of San Rio Blanco, stirring the palms and raising clouds of dust that spun in dirty swirls like ghosts at a fandango. An underfed dog barked at the stray chickens that squawked past the untended pottery booths in the market square, their feathers ruffled by the breeze as they pecked at the earth to fuel their gizzards. Pigs roamed freely, too, wrinkling their blunt snouts and squealing with abandon. Elsewhere, goats bleated from their pens and birds battled with keening insects to fill the noon air with chirps and whistles. Despite this buzz of activity, the town still reeked of emptiness and a sense of desolation. It was clear that San Rio Blanco was inhabited, but none of the townsfolk were to be seen. Doors were closed and windows were boarded, and only the most discerning gazes would have been able to see the peering, desperate eyes of those who cowered in their homes and businesses, grimly awaiting the inevitable.

They didn't have to wait for long.

From the edge of town, along the packed dirt road that

wound up from the hills, there came the whining noise of laboring engines and the creaking of worn shocks. As the sounds drew closer, the cries of birds and beasts began to fade. The pigs and chickens scrambled into hiding, and the goats turned their heads to stare down the main road that cut through the heart of town. Only the dog continued to voice its lone, pathetic protest against the coming intruders. The barks bounced off adobe storefronts and echoed throughout the village.

Then, one by one, a procession of open-topped jeeps rolled into San Rio Blanco, caked with dirt and mud from the hills and weighted down by the armed men riding within. All of the vehicles were crowded, and most of the men stood upright, shoulder to shoulder, their heads straining above the raised dust as they scanned the village for a trace of its citizens. Some had rifles slung over their shoulders or cradled in their arms; others had automatic pistols clenched tightly in their olive-skinned fists, barrels pointed outward as if in search of potential targets.

The rolling column drew to a halt near the market square, and the jeep engines idled as the dust settled. The dog snapped off one final, futile bark, then wisely scampered to the cool refuge beneath the nearest porch.

Once the church bells stopped ringing, a quiet tension claimed the air. In the lead vehicle, a thick-chested man in a khaki shirt scratched his black beard and adjusted the red bandanna that kept his wild, curly hair from spilling into his eyes. Sunlight gleamed off the gold chain dangling from his neck as he grinned savagely at the stacked pottery, the fruits and wares displayed in the market square, eyeing the items as if they were an insufficient tribute set before him in hopes of appeasing his mercurial temper. The grin gave way to a brief snort of bitter laughter, then his lips flattened and the wrath that had brought him to this town glimmered to life in his dark eyes.

"Do you think Malavida Valdez is a woman, an old witch with no teeth?!" the man roared at the townsfolk he knew were cowering within earshot. "You think he can be spit on by gringos and peasant boys? Is this the way you pay back a person who has loved you like his own *sangre*?"

A rooster crowed with false bravado across the square, but there was no other response. Valdez drew his eyebrows together and arched them into a scowl. Rage tightened his voice, spicing his words with menace. "Hey, *mis hijos* . . . it is not too late. Give to me Al Massey. Give to me this gringo snake who stirs the wind with his stinking breath. Give him to me now!"

When no one came forth to answer Valdez's demand, he glowered over his shoulder and gestured to someone in the jeep behind him. A huge, balding man stepped down from the vehicle, holding an automatic rifle pressed against the orange T-shirt that barely contained the swollen mass of his stomach. He looked to his leader with a craggy, expectant smile. When Valdez pointed to the church tower, the other man pivoted and drew aim on the steeple bells. With explosive bursts, a spray of hollow-point slugs slammed into the large bell and its smaller counterparts, scarring their surfaces and lending an unharmonious clang to the breeze.

Nearby, the dog began to howl again from the shadows beneath the porch. Valdez ignored the barking and shouted, "Come out or I will hang your gutless men and feel the warmth of your daughters while your ugly sows pour my wine!" To back up his threat, Valdez instructed his fat-bellied comrade to level his rifle and spend a round of fire on the market square. Bowls and vases shattered in the booths, and bullets skimmed across the hard ground before ripping into canvas stands and heaps of ripe fruit.

When the gunfire ceased, there was a moment's silence, then the door of the adobe house closest to Valdez creaked open. Enrique Salizon, the withered, frail mayor of San Rio Blanco, slowly stepped out onto the porch. He was humbly dressed in jeans and a bright shirt, and his fearful eyes stared out at Valdez beneath the brim of his sun-faded stetson.

"Please, *jefe*. Please," he pleaded. "We are just poor farmers. We give you everything."

"I want Al Massey!" Valdez countered. "Where is he? Where do you hide this gringo pig?"

The mayor stood trembling on the porch, clutching at his short hank of white beard as he struggled to remain silent. The other citizens of San Rio Blanco slowly began to show themselves as well, poking their heads out of doorways or through the slats of half-opened windows.

As Valdez waited for the mayor's response, the twisted smile returned to his lips. When it became clear that Enrique wasn't going to talk, Valdez let out a manic boom of laughter as he motioned for the fat man with the rifle to go over to the mayor's abode.

"Paco is requesting the pleasure of your youngest granddaughter," Valdez sneered at Enrique.

"No!" Enrique wailed with horror. "No!" He moved to one side, trying to block the steps, but Paco climbed up to the porch and effortlessly swatted the mayor to one side as he brusquely headed for the door.

"He says it would give him a great honor, amigo," Valdez shouted to his henchman. *"Toma la chica!"*

Inside the mayor's house there came a sudden shriek.

Moments later, Paco emerged, carrying a young, dark-haired woman over his shoulder. She kicked and pounded at him with her small fists, but Paco seemed oblivious to her assault and grinned happily at his leader, sharing a round of manic laughter. In the other jeeps, Valdez's minions applauded Paco's acquisition.

"He is one with the ladies, no?" Valdez taunted the mayor, who was cringing with humiliation on the porch as he watched Paco manhandle his beloved pride and joy. Turning to the larger man, Valdez called out merrily, "Hey, Paco, ask this peasant girl where is Al Massey!"

Paco was no stranger to the art of torture and interrogation, and he was deliberating a strategy for both when the young woman eliminated the need for any such tactics. At the mention of the man Malavida Valdez was seeking, her frantic gaze shifted across the plaza and lingered on a white barn the jeeps had passed on their way into town.

Al Massey scarcely looked the type of man to pose any threat to a cutthroat like Valdez. Bearing down on his sixtieth birthday, Massey was overweight and out of shape. Sweat was soaking through his shirt as he tinkered with the engine of a doorless Chevy pickup parked in the middle of the barn. A straw fedora, streaked along the brim with greasy fingerprints, was perched atop his silver hair.

"Fit, you sucker," he ordered the final screw securing the distributor cap in place. The screw eluded its mark several times before the threads finally took hold and Massey was able to twist it tightly into place.

Near the barn door several yards away, a young man stood watching through spaces in the horizontal planks, shaking his head worriedly. Unlike Massey, he was a native of the area, although his dress shirt and silk tie told of urban tastes acquired in nearby Acapulco. Glancing over his shoulder, he hissed, "Hurry Al! They're on their way!"

Massey could already hear the grinding of gears as the jeeps changed direction and started heading for the barn. Tossing aside the screwdriver, he slammed down the hood and slid in behind the wheel of the pickup. For a moment he closed his eyes and mouthed a silent prayer before starting the ignition. The engine turned over lethargically but didn't catch.

"Come on, baby, talk to me!" Massey pleaded between pumps of the accelerator. His coaxings were rewarded as the engine finally revved into life and spat a fat cloud of blue smoke out the tailpipe.

Massey's companion headed for the truck, but Al waved him away, barking, "Get outta here, Manny! Hide. He doesn't know about you."

"He'll find out," Manny said as he climbed into the passenger seat. "These people are frightened. They'll tell."

As he shifted the Chevy into first, Massey asserted, "I'm not taking you, kiddo. I already got my story, and I'm gonna write it. I don't share by-lines with anyone!"

"We'll see about that," Manny countered, bracing his hands against the dashboard. "Now let's get out of here—"

Manny's words were drowned out by the rattle of gunfire and the splintering of wood as a fusillade from the jeeps poured into the barn. Both men crouched for cover as bullets raked along the top of the truck and whistled through the glassless frame of the windshield. None of the shots found their way to the engine, though, and the truck continued to idle as Massey shifted back into neutral.

Outside the barn Valdez signaled for his men to hold

their fire, then waited for the reverberating din to subside before getting out of his jeep and taking a cautious step toward the barn. He pointed his shotgun at the riddled door before him and shouted, "Hey, Meester Massey, how 'bout you come out now, before I set fire to this whole stinking town?"

Massey could see Valdez through the door, but correctly surmised that he was still concealed from view of those outside the barn. He glanced over at Manny and gestured angrily for the Mexican to get out of the truck. Manny shook his head with equal determination.

"We talk, Meester Massey!" Valdez called out once more, softening his tone. "You will see I am but a poor country man . . . a lover of life . . . a hunter of rabbits . . . a singer of songs. We will talk. You come out. Okay?"

Shifting the truck back into gear, Massey muttered under his breath, "If this jerk hunts rabbits, it's probably with hand grenades. Well, here goes nothing . . ." Noticing that Manny's attention was focused wholly on Valdez and the barn door between them, Massey suddenly leaned over and stiff-armed his young associate, sending him tumbling out of the Chevy.

"Adios, kiddo," Massey chortled, goosing the engine as he let up on the clutch. Churning up dirt from the barn floor, the pickup lurched forward with a deafening shriek, crashing through the weakened slats of the locked door.

The sudden emergence caught Valdez off guard, and he unloosed an errant blast of his shotgun as he reeled to one side, dodging the truck like a drunken matador avoiding a wild bull. Sneering with malicious glee, Massey bore down on the nearest jeep, then cut the wheels sharply to the right just prior to collision. A shower of ammo from a dozen weapons pounded into the dirt where the truck had been.

"*Olé, muchacho!*" Valdez hailed his retreating nemesis as he rose to his feet and dusted the dirt from his breeches. Hunter that he was, he forsook his anger in favor of relishing the thrill of the chase. Bounding into his jeep, he pointed at Massey's Chevy and barked a quick order to the driver as he grabbed an automatic rifle from the man next to him and put it to use squirting lead.

Massey was in high spirits, too. He hadn't had this much fun since back in the war, when he'd commandeered a jeep through German ranks in pursuit of the stories that had earned him a reputation as one of the premier war correspondents on the European front. His reflexes weren't what they'd once been, but he had enough grit and adrenaline coursing through him to make his driving effectively reckless and unpredictable. Bounding into the market square, he maneuvered the Chevy around sharp corners, either sideswiping booths or bowling them over to make the going tough for those behind him.

"Sorry, folks," he howled crazily at the horror-stricken townspeople watching the demolition from the cover of surrounding buildings. "You'll have to put this on my tab. . . ."

More bullets smashed into the market offerings and dinged off the crumpled exterior of the pickup as Massey kept his foot down on the accelerator and tried to lengthen the distance between himself and his would-be captors. The jeep trailing closest cornered too sharply, and was launched up a ramp created by a toppled stand, flipping over with the force of its momentum and shaking free its occupants before landing, wheels upright, amidst a strewn selection of spilled produce. Valdez was in the next jeep, and he shook his head angrily at the men struggling to their feet on all sides of the disabled transport.

"Leave it for Valdez to do things right!" he yelled at them, then turned to his driver and jabbed him with the barrel of the rifle. "Catch up with that crazy Americano, Jorge, or you go back to the making of nachos, eh?"

Jorge wasn't interested in going back to the making of nachos, so he floored the jeep and barreled through a row of lightweight display stands to close the gap between his vehicle and that of the fleeing foreigner. By the time the chase had run its course through the market square and Massey was racing away from San Rio Blanco, less than twenty yards separated the hunters from the hunted. Massey hadn't been exaggerating about Valdez's hunting style, either. Bullets zinged like horizontal hail on either side of him as he negotiated the winding turns of the dirt road before him, and he was sure that the only thing that was keeping Valdez from throwing grenades at him was the fact that the Mexican probably didn't have any on him at the moment.

As he rounded a blind curve, Massey yanked hard on the steering wheel, spinning his truck about and veering up a dirt path that cut sharply away from the main road. Valdez's jeep shot past him and began braking to a halt as Massey drove off the dirt path, guiding the Chevy through a thicket and back onto the stretch of road he'd just traveled. The maneuver took the next oncoming carrier by surprise, and the driver of that vehicle jerked his wheel to avoid a collision.

"Happy landings!" Massey bade the jeep as it hurtled through another belt of shrubs and went airborne a few seconds before splashing into the middle of a large pond.

The American had little time to gloat, however. More transports were bearing down on him, spewing gunfire before them, and Valdez's jeep was already back on the scent. Massey quickly realized he had outwitted himself. He had only one avenue of escape left, and he went for it, spinning his tires and wheeling down a steep embankment that met up with the main road a few dozen yards downhill.

He didn't make it that far.

Halfway down the slope, the odds caught up with Massey and one of the stray bullets chasing him found its way through the negligible tread of the Chevy's right front tire. The tire promptly collapsed, throwing the pickup out of control. Massey gripped hard at the steering wheel, but he was unable to prevent the truck from ploughing into a clump of manzanita with so much force that the engine died on impact and Massey came close to following suit. He bounded forward sharply, then slumped back in his seat, stunned. By the time he'd come to his senses and was straggling out of the truck, his pursuers had caught up with him. Valdez glared at him triumphantly from the passenger seat of his jeep.

"You know so much about me," Valdez boasted. "You should know that no one escapes from Malavida Valdez."

Once he was out of the truck, Massey feigned nonchalance and offered Valdez and his men an ingratiating smile. "Does the tourist bureau know you guys are out here shooting up these sleepy little towns?"

Valdez shot Massey a glance that was meant to warn the American that his humor was getting him nowhere. "You make a big mistake with me, Meester Massey." Valdez got out of the jeep and slowly approached Massey, narrowing his eyes into boring slits. "How many people you tell about me? Tell me, Meester Massey. Why you come down here?"

Massey adjusted the tilt of his straw fedora, and eyed Valdez calmly and replied, "I'm on vacation . . ."

ONE

''He is *not* on vacation!''

Amy Allen fumed as she paced before the desk of her managing editor, Grant Eldridge. The window behind her provided a fourteenth story, smog-tinged view of the Los Angeles basin, where a quarter of a million copies of the morning *Courier-Express* were currently circulating. Anyone browsing the international section of the paper on any given day would find Amy's prose, either rewording wire copy or relating one of the in-depth features she sank her typewriter into once her instincts caught the scent of a story. She was twenty-five, dark-haired, and possessed with sparkling brown eyes and full lips that were equally adept at forming a disarming smile or, as was the case today, a sneer of indignation.

Eldridge had dealt with that sneer enough times to have become immune to its impact. Unhitching his loosened tie another inch, the sandy-haired man leaned forward and dispensed a baleful gaze at Amy over the rims of his bifocals. He wasn't sure what was aggravating him more today, his ulcer or his hemorrhoids. All he knew for certain was that the last thing he needed to bother himself with was the latest misadventure of Al Massey.

"Who the hell cares?" Eldridge growled. "He's on vacation or he's not. Last year we sent him to cover the French election. Did I get a story? Did I? No. He ends up lushed out of his gourd in Costa del Sol. The paper eats twenty grand in expenses, and Massey never files a word."

"That's not the point," Amy insisted, planting her hands on her hips as she met her boss's gaze.

"No, the point is you're all over the road, Allen." Eldridge swiveled in his chair and scooped up a handful of telegrams skewered on a pin holder at the edge of his desk. Adjusting his glasses, he poured over the messages. "Look, look . . . the Mexican embassy complains you threatened them . . . here's a special request from Senator Billings's office . . . and here you're using the damn paper to stir up trouble with the U.S. Senate and the Mexican government. . . ."

"I was trying to find out what happened to him," Amy countered in defense. "They claim he never entered Mexico. Damn it, Grant, doesn't this rag have a responsibility to protect its reporters on assignment?"

"Don't you give me a lecture on journalistic responsibility, sweetheart," Eldridge snapped, squirming uncomfortably on the rubber donut protecting his afflicted posterior from undue abrasion. "I was slamming adjectives up against nouns before you were on solid food! If you're looking for an early retirement, keep pressing it!"

"You can fire me, but you can't shirk your responsibility to a reporter in the field." Amy fell back to her pacing, straining the hems of her white dress with each long stride. "He was down there, trying to get a story for this paper. Something happened to him. He's missing. I don't believe you're willing to forget it."

"Well, *start* believing it," Eldridge told her, glaring

past Amy and out the window, where he could see the Goodyear blimp floating above the smog like a surfaced whale on a green sea. He took his glasses off and pressed his fingers against the bridge of his nose, trying to head off a migraine. "Listen, Al Massey has been nothing but a royal pain since he fluked into that Pulitzer two years ago. He's pissed away what little talent he had hotdogging around the globe and trying to pull stories out of a bottle. He's been doing wheels-up landings around here for over a year. I'm tired of scraping him off the front steps."

"His wife died. He's been depressed."

"Aw gee," Eldridge drawled sarcastically, "Maybe we should all chip in and buy violins and follow him around—"

"Grant . . ."

"Allen . . ." Eldridge rose from his seat, placing himself at eye level with Amy. "I've been carrying him long enough. I've had it. Yeah, he's missing, all right, but if you want my opinion, he's gonna show up in a couple of weeks wearing a lampshade at a bullfight somewhere. I'm not gonna spend any more of this paper's money on that lost cause, and I'll be damned if I'm gonna let you use the influence of this paper to rattle windows. You got that?"

The room fell silent a moment. Through the office walls could be heard the faint clatter of the teletype machine and the persistent ringing of a phone at the sports desk. Amy wrestled with her emotions, struggling to bring them under control. A deep breath finally did the job, then she offered her final argument.

"He's my friend."

It turned out to be one argument too many. Eldridge felt his migraine settling in, and he tossed aside all pretext of patience. Circling around his desk, he told Amy flatly, "You need some time off, Allen. I'm suspending you on half pay for two weeks. You're a good reporter, but you're going to have to learn how to stop sitting on your brains. Turn your feature stuff over to Mark and file your filler before you leave.''

Amy was stunned. "Just like that . . .''

Eldridge headed for the mini-cooler across the room. Before opening it, he looked back at Amy and pointed to the door. "Honey, get out before I pull your plug all the way.''

It came out as a friendly warning, but did little to soften the blow. Amy's lips tightened as she fought back the bevy of retorts that were clamoring to be spoken. She knew that any back talk at this stage would cost her her job. As Eldridge turned his back to her and took a carton of milk out of the cooler to soothe his ulcer, she went for the door and let herself out.

Eldridge's office opened out into the city room, a maze of makeshift partitions and desks cluttered with notes and every type of writing implement from pad and pencil on up to industrial strength typewriters and the newest crop of scanner-screen word processors. There was a lull in the action as the assembled staff watched Amy emerge from her confrontation with Eldridge. She flinched at all the attention, and a rosy blush spread across her face as her co-workers suddenly greeted her with a patter of light applause.

Bill Zachary, the youngest member of the *Courier* staff after Amy, broke away from the others and beamed proudly at his colleague, telling her, "Somebody had to say it.''

The applause was dying down when the office door swung open once more and Eldridge looked out at his crew. There was no need for him to speak. The staff immediately gravitated back to work, avoiding their editor's stern gaze. He remained in the doorway a few seconds longer, then retreated to his desk to await the anticipated relief of the Excedrin and Valium he'd washed down with his first sip of milk.

As Amy headed out of the city room, she was treated to a few more high signs and thumbs up. Bill Zachary stayed on her heels and followed her out into the corridor leading to their office. He was half a head shorter than her but walked with a bouncing stride that seemed to compensate. His designer glasses were perched on a large nose hovering just above a wide grin that seemed on the verge of splitting his face in half.

"That was really great," he enthused, "telling that fathead about journalistic responsibility."

Amy wasn't in the mood for compliments, though. As they headed down the hallway, passing blowups of front pages depicting the *Courier*'s coverage of the greater headlines of the century, she asked, "Did you find Massey's research notes, Zack? Did he file any copy?"

"Nothing," Zachary confessed. The grin stayed on his face, however, and when they entered the cramped quarters of the international room, he beelined to his desk. "I found nothing here, but I took the liberty of stopping by his house. You see, I did a little second-story work when I was on the *Miami Herald*. I'm a killer with louvered windows. I went through his apartment last night, and I managed to find this file under his mattress."

"Where are your ethics, Zack?" Amy asked as she plucked the file from his hands and opened it. "Thanks."

"Don't mention it."

The index tab on the file read "SAN RIO BLANCO." Inside the file was nothing but a scrap of paper with a name and number scrawled hastily in almost indecipherable handwriting. Amy frowned and looked up at Zachary. "Manny Cortez? San Rio Blanco? And what's this, a phone number?"

"I think so," Zachary told her. "I looked up San Rio Blanco. It's a town way up in the hills above Acapulco."

"Wonderful," Amy groaned dismally. "If I was the CIA, I might have a one-in-a-million chance of getting anywhere on a lead like this." She set the file down and sank into the chair at her desk, letting out a sigh of resignation.

"Sorry, Aim," Zachary offered as he leaned against the side of her desk. "I wish there was more."

"You did what you could, Zack. I appreciate it." Amy ran her fingers through her hair, then reached over for the stack of feature-stories-in-progress filed in a wire basket next to Zachary. "Well, I guess all I can do now is to pass along this stuff and then catch a flight to . . . wait!"

Amy sat suddenly upright, and her eyes glimmered with excitement as she pulled aside one of the other files.

"What? What is it?" Zachary asked her, glancing down at the folder Amy was so engrossed with. It was even less filled than Massey's San Rio Blanco file. In fact, there was nothing in the folder at all. The index tab read merely "MERCENARIES."

"Zack, what about that commando team, or whatever . . . did you find out anything more about them?"

Zachary could sense the gears working inside Amy's head, and he didn't like the direction he thought they were taking her. He shook his head disapprovingly and advised, "I told ya, Aim, it's rumor. Strictly a rumor. Even if they *did* exist, you'd be outta your mind to go—"

"I'll be the judge of that, Zack," Amy snapped, "just let me in on what you know, okay?"

Zachary hesitated a moment, searching for an effective argument. He saw the determination in Amy's eyes but still tried to dissuade her. "Mike Kelly tried to trace that story six months ago, before he got sacked, but he couldn't even prove they existed. There was a rumor, quote 'rumor,' that they broke some Senator's kid out of a Turkish prison. It's all real vague how the kid actually got out. Deadendsville, know what I mean?"

If Amy knew what Zachary meant, she didn't seem ready to admit it. Her face was filled with hope. "The A-Team," she recalled, "that's what he called them."

Zachary nodded, rolling his eyes. "The A-Team. Soldiers of fortune. Outriders," he said with increasingly mock exaggeration. "Counterculture nutburgers who'll do anything, anywhere if the price is right. That was the rumor. Kelly had a theory on who they were, but, like I said, he ran out of leads by the time he got canned, and the whole mess ended up in the research library."

Amy sprang from her seat, saying, "I've tried all the conventional alternatives. Bring on the counterculture nutburgers!" She headed for the door, waving the empty file as she bade Zachary to follow her. "Come on, this folder's hungry . . ."

TWO

"THREE-MAN COMMANDO TEAM
ROB HANOI BANK: ARMY
SETS COURT-MARTIAL"

The newsclipping was faded and yellow, but the headline still flashed boldly across the top of the story from an old issue of the *Courier*.

"These guys knocked over the Bank of Hanoi," Zachary was telling Amy as he stabbed his finger at the folder containing the clipping. They were in the dimly lit research library, located on the twelfth floor of the building adjacent to the office of the sports editor, who could be heard throwing darts at an 8 x 10 glossy of Grant Eldridge and cheering whenever he scored a direct hit.

"That's what the headline says, all right," Amy said glibly. "How about the gory details?"

"Happened four days before we pulled out of Vietnam," Zachary explained. "They wandered out of the DMZ with a hundred million yen and got busted by the Army. Their story was that they acted under orders from some colonel named Morrison, but Morrison took a round in one of the last shellings and his headquarters burned to the ground.''

"Hmmmmm. Sounds suspicious.''

"That's the way the Army looked at it, too,'' Zachary went on. "No records of any orders for such a mission turned up, and nobody vouched for these guys who got caught. The Hanoi government was screaming bloody murder. The Pentagon wanted to soothe tempers, so they set up plans for a major court-martial. Apparently the commandos weren't on anyone's list of favorite people, so the skids were being greased for a quick conviction. They must have known the score because a few days before the trial they went over the wall at Fort Bragg and disappeared.''

"Disappeared? Poof, just like that?'' Amy frowned.

Zachary nodded. "And that was ten years ago.''

Through the wall Amy and Zachary heard the sports editor exult in a bull's-eye.

Amy mulled over the folder a moment, trying to get a perspective on the three men and how they might fit into her plans for finding Al Massey. She was beginning to have her doubts. "They're still wanted?'' she asked Zachary.

"Yup.'' Zachary wandered over to the bank of filing cabinets huddled together the length of the far wall. As he scanned the headings on various drawers for the one he sought, he called out over his shoulder, "There's a guy in here, a colonel named Lynch . . . he ran the prison at Fort Bragg . . . took a lot of heat for letting them get away. Cost him a promotion or two over the years . . . ah, here it is!'' He yanked out still another file and brought it over to Amy, showing her a color shot of a dour-faced man staring out at the world with the look of someone burdened with a grudge. He had a square jaw and a thick, reddish moustache that looked like a pregnant caterpillar doing yoga on his upper lip.

"Looks like the guy who modeled for the original Happy Face," Amy smirked. "He could pass for Eldridge's kid brother."

"He's still trying to find the guys," Zachary said. "It's a personal vendetta for him. But, like I said, they disappeared ten years ago, and they aren't taking out any ads."

"Okay, Zack, I'm sufficiently intrigued," Amy said, turning her attention back to the other file and flipping past the old newsclipping to a series of photos. "Who are these guys?"

The first photo was of a man with silvering hair and light eyes that betrayed an impish twinkle more befitting the face of the senior class cutup. "Colonel John Smith," Zachary identified him. "Everyone called him Hannibal. The guy has real unorthodox style."

"Not bad," Amy murmured, raising an eyebrow. "Where'd he come from?"

"Nobody knows for sure. He claimed different roots on every form he filled out. Most people guess he's from the Midwest somewhere. Even the Army doesn't have much on him that they can verify, which is kinda strange all by itself."

"Maybe they weren't being that picky when he joined up," Amy suggested. "Who else?"

Zachary pulled aside Hannibal's photo, revealing a mug shot of a mean-faced black man whose head was shaved except for sideburns and a tight-curled Mohawk. "Bosco Baracus . . . known as B.A. for short."

"B.A.?" Amy asked, shuddering slightly at the fierce expression on the black man's face.

"Bad Attitude."

"I can see that. . . ."

"He had a reputation as best field infantry mechanic in Nam. He's a mechanical genius, but he had one of the worst conduct records in the Army. Seems he had a fondness for slugging officers."

"Terrific."

The last picture was of a young, handsome man with a self-confident smile pressed across his face. He looked like someone who'd be more comfortable in a Brooks Brothers suit than fatigues.

"This is more like it," Amy said, smiling back at the man in the photo.

"Templeton Peck," Zachary explained. "They call him the Face Man, in case you hadn't guessed. An orphan from L.A. Grew up in and out of trouble. This guy is Mister Ricky-Ticky. A con man, a real operator."

"Sounds like half the men I meet at bars," Amy claimed, eyeing Peck a final time before closing the file.

"That's the unit, save for some guy named Murdock who did some flying for them in Nam. He's a mental case now, though. Lives at the Vets' hospital," Zachary said. "As for the others, where they are these days is anybody's guess. Kelly couldn't stumble on anything but rumors before Eldridge put him out to pasture. No facts. Zip. Story's been on ice here in the morgue since then."

"Well, I'm just going to have to defrost it, then," Amy said, rolling up the file and slipping it into her purse.

"Taking a working vacation, then, are you?"

Amy nodded. "Not a word of this to Eldridge, though."

"Gotcha," Zachary said as they left the library and headed down the hall to the elevators.

Amy pressed the down button. As they waited she stared thoughtfully into space, then whispered to herself, "I wonder where they are now."

THREE

The lake was calm and clear, its surface gleaming like taut Saran Wrap under the afternoon sun. Flies buzzed lazily above the mirrored water while their land-bound cousins rubbed their legs together along the shore, making music. Inspired, a pair of bullfrogs cleared their throats and rehearsed for their nightly serenade. Small schools of fish flitted amidst the algae dangling upward from the lake bottom, and thousands of tadpoles scurried about like errant commas, busying themselves along the metamorphic road to froghood. This wasn't Walden, or even Golden Pond, but the overwhelming atmosphere seemed to be that of peaceful tranquility, the kind of surroundings harried urbanites might flock to in hopes of shedding stress and worry like dead skin in molting season.

Then the creature appeared.

It rose without warning from the shallow depths of the lake, breaking the water's surface and heading for shore. It had the scaly, grotesque features of a dragon, with long yellow fangs, flaring nostrils, and large, reptilian eyes that bore a disturbing glint of intelligence. Water rolled off its greenish flesh as it continued to emerge from its lair, revealing a long neck and broad shoulders. The laws of physiology dictated that the body of such a creature should be that of an elongated quadruped, and yet it cleared the pitched slope of the embankment on its hind legs alone, then began advancing along the earthen terrain with an awkwardness that was only partially due to the long, rounded tail that dragged behind it. From the neck down its dimensions were blatantly humanoid, and whatever pretense of horror the monster might have initially suggested was quickly dispelled by the penguinish waddle with which it advanced. With each passing second it looked more like a costumed wino on the way to the Mardi Gras than a threat to anyone's life and limb.

A second disruption to the serenity came in the form of a screeching Rambler convertible that raised a trail of dust along the dirt road leading down to the lake from the surrounding hillside. Two people were seated inside the swerving vehicle. The passenger was light-skinned, with the kind of groomed hair that would have looked wind-blown even if the roof was up. The driver's ebony flesh was encrusted with gold jewelry that shone brightly in the sunlight. His corded biceps knotted as he wrestled with the steering wheel, rounding a corner and then slamming on the brakes.

Templeton Peck rose in his seat and peered downhill before telling B.A., "He's gotta be down there somewhere. Let's go!"

B.A. sneered as he eased down on the accelerator and urged the Rambler along the steep road leading to the lake. The Face Man sat back down and held on for dear life.

"Cut! *Cut!*" An angry voice carried across the lake from the vicinity of the monster. "Who the hell is that?!"

The exclamation had come from a goateed movie director who launched himself from his folding chair and clutched angrily at the beret he'd yanked from his head as he pointed to the approaching car. He was surrounded by a film crew of several dozen people manning everything from clipboards with shooting scripts to huge crane-operated cameras. The filming had been beset by complications all day, and this latest snag was greeted by a variety of grumbles and profanities. Behind the small army of technicians, the pastoral backdrop gave way to an old western set and then to other precariously standing facades that marked the fringe of the Universal Studios shooting lot. Gathered together in these few rambling acres was all the necessary scenery to film everything from tropical paradises to extraterrestrial battle zones. Hollywood.

As he strode angrily toward his assistant, the director howled, "Where'd that moron come from?!" Snatching the other man's walkie-talkie, he roared on, "Hey, Mike, don't we have someone up on that road to hold traffic, damn it?"

"Sorry, Jerry," came the tinny response over the small speaker on the walkie-talkie. "Our screw-up. We'll get a guy up there."

The director handed back the communicator and shook his head with disgust. Planting the beret back on his head and adjusting it so that it tilted without mussing his toupee, he walked over to the creature from the pond, which was standing with its hands on its hips. "Come on, come on, people!" he shouted to the crew, "Let's be alert for a change, okay? We're losing the light here."

The creature had a trapdoor where its Adam's apple was, and when the director yanked the door open, Hannibal Smith grinned out at him, his face framed by the opening. A script girl wandered over and placed a thin cigar between Hannibal's lips. It was already lit, and Hannibal blew smoke. From a distance it looked like the dragon had just had a tracheotomy and was exhaling through its neck.

"Johnny . . . I want thirty seconds under water," the director told Hannibal firmly. "Thirty seconds after 'Action.' You're popping up like the rubber duck in my kid's bathtub."

Hannibal squinted disbelievingly. "Thirty seconds? You nuts?! I gotta stay down there two minutes to let the water get still . . . then thirty seconds after that?"

Over the director's shoulder Hannibal could see the Rambler clear a final turn and begin barreling toward the film crew. He smiled when he recognized the men in the front seat.

"Hey, pal, that's the job," the director was lecturing him. "We woulda got Sir Laurence Olivier, but he didn't fit in the suit, so we settled for you. Your agent said you could stay down three and a half minutes. Hell, in *Aquamania I* we had a guy who stayed down for four minutes."

"Why isn't he doing it now?" Hannibal wondered.

"He had a little brain hemorrhage or something . . . I don't know," the director complained. "Anyway, let's go. Let's get this sucker in the can." He pointed past Hannibal to the pond and ordered, "Back in the drink, chickie." Heading back to his folding throne, he told the others, "Same shot. Camera, position one."

Before shooting had a chance to resume, though, B.A. wheeled the old Rambler into the midst of the production and the Face Man bounded out of the car, shouting to no one in particular, "I'm looking for John Smith. John? John? Where are ya, John?"

Hannibal shuffled in his burdensome outfit and waved a scaly arm to get the Face Man's attention. "Here," he growled around his cigar.

"Get back in the lake!" the director commanded, reaching for the megaphone next to his chair as if it were a bazooka that was going to help back up his wishes. "Who do ya think you are, Gloria Swanson? Let's go. I'm on a tight clock here!"

The Face Man ignored the director and rushed over to Hannibal, gasping, "He's onto us, Hannibal! Colonel Lynch. He hit B.A.'s pad two hours ago with six M.P.'s. They were parked out in front of my place like a buncha goonies at a supermarket opening."

Hannibal gingerly plucked the cigar from his lips with his costumed hand, which was the size of a baseball glove. "How'd he trace us?" he asked Peck.

"I don't know," the Face Man said. "Maybe the senator's son talked. I never thought that kid had all his lights on."

Hannibal frowned. "If the kid burned us, then Lynch probably knows about me doing this."

"You got it, Tonto," Peck said. "I think we should disappear, like right now."

The director bellowed through his megaphone, "Would the Aquamaniac please tear himself away from his boyfriend and get back in the damn lake?!"

Hannibal looked at the Face Man with resignation as he drew in a final puff of smoke and then tossed aside his cigar. "I got one more shot, then I'm through. Watch this. I think I got a real handle on my character here," he mused philosophically. "I'm playing him mean, but with a kinda sad reluctance."

As Hannibal was jockeying around to head back for the water, Face glanced up the way he and B.A. had arrived on the scene. "You're about to get a chance to play it for Colonel Lynch, Hannibal."

Up the hill three sleek black limousines were on the scent of the Rambler's tracks. They slowed along a clearing overlooking the lake, and the front window on the lead car rolled down long enough for Colonel Lynch to poke his head out and jab a pointing finger down at the set. If the finger had been loaded, he could have been a dragonslayer. "That's him, in the lizard suit!" he shouted. "John Hannibal Smith. Get him!"

As the three limos picked up speed and headed downhill, passengers in each vehicle reached out and placed portable flashers on the shining roofs. Red lights began to blink and whirl, and sirens screamed into life, further shattering the illusion of peace around the lake.

B.A. Baracus's mechanical expertise had been put to good use on the Rambler, and when he shifted gears and sped over to Face Man and Hannibal, it was a Corvette engine that sounded its mighty roar beneath the hood. This was a machine that was meant to move.

"Where are you going?" the director called out when he saw Hannibal follow the Face Man into the convertible.

"Waldorf Astoria, driver," Hannibal told B.A., grinning as he settled into the back seat of the Rambler and pulled his tail in behind him. "And step on it."

"Funny," B.A. growled, putting his foot to the floor. The Rambler responded by bolting forward, its spinning tires spitting gravel back at the three limousines that had just reached level ground. As the film crew gawked with wonder, the chase began in earnest.

"This is *not* in the script!" the director whined. "Why me? Why is this happening to me? I've been a good—"

"*Aquamania III!*" his assistant suddenly blurted out.

"We should be filming this, and then we can write a script around it for the next sequel!"

The director's expression changed as dramatically as if he'd just heard God. Waving his arms frantically, he pointed to the receding vehicles and shouted to the cameramen, "Action! Zoom in, pan, whatever! Get this on film! Yes! This is genius!"

"Thanks, boss," his assistant called out above the commotion.

"What are you talking about?" Getting his hands on the nearest walkie-talkie, the director snapped off a quick request for his second unit, which was filming on the other side of the lot, to be on the lookout for the Aquamaniac. When asked for details, the director yelled, "No time for that. I only just now had the brainstorm! Just do it!"

The Universal back lot was not strictly the province of film crews. For years the studio had added to its coffers by loading tourists on trams for tours of the facilities and a glimpse at the inner workings behind the blockbusters of yesterday and tomorrow. One such tram was rolling slowly past the western set while a guide spewed forth her rehearsed bevy of trivia-laden anecdotes.

". . . and whereas, to the viewer, it looks as if all of these buildings are completely constructed, from our perspective you can see that, in fact, only . . . what?!!"

B.A. veered the Rambler around a corner and onto the same dusty street as the tram, startling the guide into dumbfounded silence. As the convertible whisked past, there was mass activity aboard the tram as several dozen cameras were raised and hastily focused on the absurd figure of Hannibal Smith riding in the back seat.

"Mommie, Mommie!" one of the younger children in the tram shouted excitedly. "It's the Aquamaniac!"

Hannibal beamed at his audience and waved like a politician in a ticker tape parade. "Hi there," he called out cheerfully.

"I ain't stopping for no autographs, Hannibal," B.A. snarled as he drove by.

"Shucks," Hannibal moaned.

"Maybe you oughta close your face," Peck suggested, reaching for the trapdoor in the neck of Hannibal's costume. "Some of these kids are gonna think you're something the Aquamaniac ate that didn't agree with him."

"No way," Hannibal said, swatting away the Face Man's hand. "The way B.A.'s driving, this might be the last drive I ever take. I want to at least see where I'm going."

"We're goin' to Chicago, sucker," B.A. said, checking the rearview mirror to see how close Lynch's men were before squealing around a stagecoach and heading down a paved street flanked by old brownstones and other building facades approximating the Windy City around the time of Prohibition. This set was vacant, and B.A. made use of side streets to put more distance between them and their pursuers.

"There's a speakeasy," Hannibal said, taking in the scenery. "Why don't we stop for a sip of something tall and cool?"

"Nothin' doin'," B.A. countered, leaning over the steering wheel as he wove the car around a parked ice truck and off the Chicago lot to a wilderness setting sliced by a gurgling stream. His fancy driving had proved too slick for his own good, though, as he had brought them back into view of the speeding limos, which bore down on the Rambler with grim intent.

B.A. sought out a ramp and revved the engine to propel the convertible over the stream.

"Weeee, we're flying!" the Face Man shouted, bracing himself in the front seat.

"Shut up!" B.A. snapped. "You know I *hate* to fly!"

"Sorry."

The convertible touched down and kept going, racing on a course parallel to that of Bruce, the mechanical shark terrorizing another tramful of tourists passing by the *Jaws* set.

"How about *Jaws versus the Aquamaniac*?" Hannibal thought aloud. "It's a natural!"

"Quit jokin', Hannibal!" B.A. said over his shoulder. "This ain't no picnic we're on!"

Face turned in his seat and looked past Hannibal in time to see the limousines trying to vault the stream. Only one of them made it. The other two plopped into the mire of the creekbed and stayed put. Colonel Lynch leaned out of the remaining vehicle and shook a fist at Face.

"Colonel Lynch doesn't look too happy," he told Hannibal. "I think he's trying to tell us to say our prayers."

"Holy Moses!" Hannibal quipped, suddenly inspired. "B.A., let's check out the Red Sea!"

"You got it!" B.A. cornered the Rambler and laid rubber across the lot to where still another tram had almost completed its trek across the severed expanse of lake Charlton Heston had led his flock through in the climax of *The Ten Commandments*, its waters hovering at either side of the passageway. The A-Team temporarily joined the chosen people and cleared the parted waters, too, then Hannibal signaled for B.A. to stop the car.

"What you goin' to do, Hannibal?"

"Now, B.A., I wouldn't want to spoil the surprise,"

Hannibal said as he lugged his padded frame out of the convertible and waddled over to the machinery that worked the Red Sea. A large lever activated by the passage of the tram was slowly creaking forth to close the break in the waters. Hannibal yanked the lever back and the clearing remained.

"Whatta ya doin', Hannibal?" Face Man yelled. "Pull it and let's make tracks!"

Hannibal smirked back at his allies and shook his head. Moments later, the pursuing limousine sped into view, heading for the sea. Colonel Lynch saw Hannibal manning the switch and immediately screamed at his driver, "Stop! Stop!"

The driver stood on the brakes and the limousine swung to one side as it stopped a few yards shy of the partition in the sea. Lynch opened his door and got out, staring at Hannibal with confusion.

"What's he doing?" he asked his driver.

"Beats me. He's a lizard, for crying out loud."

Across the way, Face Man was having fits. Cupping his hands over his mouth, he cried out, "Pull it already, Hannibal. Let's go!"

B.A. scowled, shaking his head as he watched Hannibal. "He ain't pulling it yet, Face. He loves the risk, the danger. Damn fool loves that jazz."

Hannibal and Lynch stared at one another for what seemed to be an eternity. Their eyes shared looks of intense concentration, but the rest of their faces were completely different. While Lynch's features were contorted into an expression suggesting advanced constipation, Hannibal was clearly enjoying himself. A vixen smile was splashed across his face as he pulled his hand off the lever and curled a dragon finger invitingly toward him.

"He's daring us," Lynch surmised, tensing alongside the limousine.

Hannibal took one step away from the lever, then another, assuming a partial stance similar to a ballplayer taking a lead off first base. Considering the uniform he was wearing, he wasn't much of a threat to lead any league in stolen bases, though.

"Come on, you big, ugly pile of crud," Lynch seethed under his breath. "One more step . . . just one more."

Hannibal obliged, putting ten full yards between himself and the lever.

"Okay, now!" Lynch slipped back inside the limousine, and the driver put the accelerator to the floor.

Simultaneously, Hannibal swaggered clumsily back to the lever. His monstrous fingers closed around the handle just as the limousine roared into the chasm between the two bodies of water. Before the car could clear the full distance, Hannibal threw the switch, and the two walls of water charged into one another, catching the limousine in the middle. Its forward progress was immediately halted. The waters buoyed up the vehicle momentarily, then pulled it under. With great difficulty Lynch and his driver managed to open their doors and abandon the limousine. The water level was up to their necks, though, and they bounced awkwardly on their tiptoes trying to stay afloat.

Watching them from the safety of dry land, Hannibal let out a long laugh. He waited until he had Lynch's attention, then chortled, "I guess you aren't Moses, Colonel, but nice try anyway. . . ."

Lynch spat out a mouthful of water, then clambered up onto the hood of the submerged limousine, where he glared at Hannibal and once more aimed his unloaded finger at Hannibal's heart. "Laugh now while you can, but I swear you'll pay for this, just like you'll pay for the past ten years you've put me through.''

"It's not nice to point," Hannibal called out as he wave to the two uniformed men now struggling atop the sunken car. "If we see anybody with some soap, we'll send 'em by to help you out. That limo should look right spiffy once it gets out of the wash. Ta da . . . !''

B.A. was tired of waiting for Hannibal to rejoin them, so he put the Rambler into reverse and backed up, then called out, "Get your butt in here, Hannibal, or I'm leavin' you behind.''

Hannibal came over and wrangled himself back into the rear seat, then fumbled inside the seat pocket for a fresh cigar. He poked it in his mouth as B.A. drove off.

"Damn it, Hannibal," the Face Man complained as they headed away from the back lot and on down the road leaving the studio. "All you had to do was pull the lever. What was all that Maury Wills junk? He coulda fired a shot or blown a wheel off this bus and botched our getaway.''

"Good point," Hannibal said with mock earnestness. "Got a match up there?''

B.A. forced a grin as he punched in the dashboard lighter. "Ol' Hannibal loves the jazz, man," he told Face again. "He loves the jazz.''

"Come on, you guys, lighten up," Hannibal said, leaning back in his seat, pleased with himself. "You gotta do these things with some style. Don't tell me you didn't love seein' him up to his chin in rancid water.''

The lighter popped out of the dash slightly. B.A. took it the rest of the way out and held it over his shoulder while Hannibal lit up his cigar. "Man, you're one crazy piece of work, sucker.''

"Why, thank you, Bosco," Hannibal said, blowing a smoke ring. "Nice of you to say that."

The Face Man paused a moment to consider these men he ran around with. A maniac dressed as a dragon and a mean thug who wore jewelry and a Mohawk. "I've got to be out of my mind," he finally decided.

They were now approaching the main gates to the studio. A uniformed guard stepped out from the security booth and scrutinized the car, then flashed a smile and waved them by.

"Have a nice one, Mr. Smith," the guard told Hannibal.

"You too, Scotty," Hannibal called out.

As B.A. turned onto Lankershim and headed for the freeway, Face repeated, "I've got to be out of my mind. . . ."

FOUR

Half an hour later the A-Team was cruising Hollywood Boulevard, choking on the blue-black exhaust of a tourist bus inching its way toward the curb in front of Mann's Chinese Theatre. Billboards touting new movies, books, and record albums sprouted from the tops of buildings infested with neon signs awaiting the coming darkness for a chance to show off their gaudy colors; the sidewalks were inlaid with gilded stars bearing the names of entertainment greats, but the celebrities themselves were nowhere to be seen. It had been years since this stretch had embodied anything remotely suggesting glamour, and tourists straying too far from their busses in search of excitement were more apt to find it in the form of crime or vice than in a glimpse at the next Lana Turner sucking on a cherry cola at Schwab's. Transients, shysters, crooks, and conmen roamed freely through the pedestrian traffic, keeping one eye open for potential victims or clients and the other for the first sign of a patrol car or undercover agent from the city's vice squad. In short, Hollywood Boulevard was one of the few places the three men in the Rambler could drive through without drawing undue attention.

Or so they thought.

When B.A. pulled into a parking space and the Face Man hopped out to grab some food at the nearest takeout stand, a flock of wide-eyed out-of-towners poured out of the tourist bus and wandered over to the Rambler, training their cameras on Hannibal. One shy woman wriggled her way through the mob, child in tow, and cleared her throat nervously before asking, "Excuse me, but are you the Aquamaniac?"

Hannibal nodded slightly, tipping the monster's head toward the woman as if it were contemplating making a meal of her. "That's right," he said proudly, loud enough for the others to hear. "I am the Aquamaniac."

"Could we have your autograph?"

"I'd be delighted."

Simultaneously, a dozen hands shot outward, shoving everything from paper napkins to maps of stars' homes in Hannibal's face. Hannibal took a pen from one of the people and struggled to get a good grip on it with his creature fingers before flourishing signatures across the scraps of paper.

"This is crazy," B.A. said. "We're on the lam and you're bein' a hot dog."

"The Aquamaniac is not a hot dog," Hannibal insisted between autographs. "He's a metaphor for the primal fears of man as embodied in the collective subconscious."

"Jive," B.A. muttered, shaking his head.

The Face Man returned, circling around the crowd and climbing into the car with a takeout bag already pocked with grease stains from its quick-fried contents. "Let's hit it, B.A. I heard an A.P.B. come out for us on the walkie-talkie of the cop in line behind me. I'm lucky he didn't recognize me."

"See ya in the pictures!" Hannibal called out to his adoring fans as B.A. pulled the Rambler back out into the flow of traffic.

The Face Man passed around chili dogs and cheeseburgers, saying, "What we gonna do, Hannibal?"

"Yeah," B.A. grumbled, weaving through traffic and turning onto a side street leading up into the Hollywood Hills. "I mean, we can't even go home or nothin'!"

"Okay, okay," Hannibal said between bites of his burger. For the first time since the day's chase began, an expression of seriousness crossed his face. "First thing we gotta do is warn Murdock. If Lynch is onto us, he's probably caught a whiff of Murdock, too."

"Murdock," B.A. growled. "Best thing that could happen is if that peanut head was to get locked up."

"He *is* locked up," Hannibal reminded B.A. "Let's track down a phone booth so I can give him a call."

B.A. spotted a booth behind a gas station at the end of the block and changed lanes before pulling up in front of it. As he turned off the engine, he looked at Hannibal in the rearview mirror and said, "With everybody looking for us, why don't you go change outta that lizard suit before you call? Man, you stick out like a sore thumb!"

"Look who's talking," Hannibal said, flicking his finger at the cluster of necklaces dangling from B.A.'s shoulders, then pointing to the black man's Mohawk.

"I'm gettin' mad," B.A. warned.

"Just calm down, B.A.," Hannibal said, opening the back door and squirming out of the Rambler. "It'll be all right. Count on it."

B.A. stared at the ludicrous figure of Hannibal making his way to the phone booth. He chomped on his chili dog, devouring half of it in one bite, then washed it down with a long draw of root beer. After wiping his mouth with a napkin, he looked over at the Face Man and said, "How long we been doing this now?"

"Doing what, B.A.?"

"You know what I'm talkin' about. Livin' on the run all the time. Hidin' out in the underground; always having that turkey Lynch breathin' down our necks. . . ."

"Oh, that. A long time, B.A. A long time."

"Yeah, too long if you ask me."

"Hey, it's not that bad. Come on, you gotta admit it's nice to feel wanted, right?"

"Funny man," B.A. said, finishing off his dog.

The Face Man punched B.A. playfully on the bicep. "You love it, B.A., and you know it. Just like Hannibal, you love the jazz. That's why we all get along so well."

"We don't get along, sucker. You know that."

The Face Man turned his smile upside down. "Hey, man, what are you trying to do, hurt my feelings?"

"You keep buggin' me, Face, I'm gonna hurt more than your feelings."

The Face Man grinned again. "Anyone tell you you're ugly when you're mad, B.A.?"

"Spare me the flattery, sucker." B.A. tried to scowl, but the corners of his mouth were turning up, curling like cobras under the spell of a flute-playing fakir.

FIVE

They called him Howling Mad Murdock for good reason.

His current residence was the psychiatric wing of the Veterans' Administration Hospital in West Los Angeles, where he was under observation and treatment for various strains of cerebral maladjustments. Doctors attempting to pigeonhole him into any one psychological profile had quickly discovered that consistency was not one of Murdock's stronger traits. Like a television set with its channel selector on the fritz, Murdock had a tendency to flick from one set of symptoms to another without warning or seeming provocation. He could be a manic-depressive one moment and a slavering psychotic the next, all the while carrying on a wavering monologue that defied either logic or comprehension. Trying to keep up with his stream of consciousness required the mental equivalent of white water rafting. There were those at the hospital who claimed Murdock was nothing more than a poseur going through the motions of instability, but they had no way of proving their suspicions, and since he was basically harmless and didn't subject the staff to too much hardship or harassment, he was allowed to spend most of his time alone in his room, amusing himself as he saw fit.

When Amy Allen was ushered into Murdock's room that afternoon by a prim-looking nurse, Howling Mad was busily absorbed with one of the several video games lining the walls. Hunched over the screen, his back turned to Amy, he bobbed and weaved to the accompaniment of electronic-sounding blips and blams, cheering himself on or spouting manic warnings to the imaginary enemies on the grid before him.

"Good luck, honey, he's all yours," the nurse said, smiling stiffly at Amy's nervousness. "Don't worry, he's seldom violent. If he gets out of hand, just mention ammonia and head for the door and you'll be okay."

" 'Mention ammonia and head for the door,' " Amy repeated, increasingly uncertain about what she was getting herself into. As the nurse backtracked and closed the door behind her, Amy walked quietly toward Murdock, clutching tightly to her clipboard as if it were a shield.

The noise emanating from Murdock's side of the room kept him distracted, and Amy had a chance to observe him more closely without him taking notice of her. He was tall and thin, in his late twenties, although a hastily receding hairline made him look several years older. He was wearing moccasins and jeans and a black T-shirt with the name "Napoleon" emblazoned across his chest. As Amy came up beside him, she saw that his eyes were the most telling thing about him. They were large and dark, constantly on the move, like a pair of intelligent marbles trying to look for a way out of the heavy-lidded sockets holding them prisoner.

Amy also noticed that the video game Murdock was playing wasn't plugged in. There was nothing on the screen but his dark reflection. The cacophony of noises weren't coming from the machine, but rather from his constantly moving lips.

"Rippa rippa . . . bbbbbbrap bbbbbbrappppp . . . KACHEENG KACHEENG!" Murdock babbled, "Take that, fiendish android mongers! Haha! Zzzzzzzzzzap . . . chunga chunga . . . Attaway, Luke! Bring on the Death Ray if you must, vile . . ."

Murdock's voice trailed off as he caught sight of Amy out of the corner of his eye. He turned to her and smiled charmingly, then calmly said, in an accent that sounded Italian by way of Brooklyn, "Ah gotta no qwahtahs, Mamma, but Ah just gotta getta mah kicks, 'ayyyyy?"

Amy returned the smile and said, "I guess it cuts down on your power bill, too, right?"

Murdock stood stiffly upright and slapped his forehead. "Mamma mia. My power pill!" Two long strides took him across the room to the sink next to his bed. He grabbed a phial from the medicine cabinet and bit off the child-proof cap before tapping out a capsule the size of a jelly bean into his palm. Glancing back at Amy, he grinned and declared, "Ees one magic bean, Mamma. Onally costa me two cows."

"How nice," Amy said, struggling to remain calm and veer the conversation back on track. "Maybe if you plant it and give it lots of water, it'll grow as high as a helicopter flies."

Murdock popped the pill in his mouth, then cupped his hands under running water and lapped up a quick drink. When he stood back up, he sucked in his stomach, letting his chest expand. He pounded it with both fists before announcing, "Mmmmmm, good pill. Give Murdock power of great ape."

"More like the power of great bull," Amy said. "Or maybe even 'A-Team' of bulls, hmmm, Murdock?"

"Say what?" For a split second the madness fled from Murdock's face, and his eyebrows arched with suspicion.

Amy spotted the change and threw in another hint. "Forget bulls. I'll bet it makes you as powerful as a herd of elephants."

Murdock stabbed his hands into his pockets and retreated into a cowboy persona, drawling, "Heck, yes, ma'am, Ah heard of elephants. Look like a big mouse with a long nose, ain't that so?"

"Something like that," Amy said. "I remember reading in my history book about how Hannibal used them to cross the Alps. You know about Hannibal, don't you, Murdock?"

Murdock exhaled, blowing out his alter egos in the process. "Who are you?" he asked.

"Amy Allen. I work for the L.A. *Courier-Express*, and a friend of mine who works the international beat has disappeared in Mexico while on assignment. I want to hire the A-Team to find him. I've checked around and I know you're associated with them, so if you could quit playing Rich Little with a lobotomy and give me some answers, I'd appreciate it." She rattled off the speech in one breath, then stared with wonder at Murdock as if amazed at her performance.

Murdock didn't answer at first. He continued to stare at Amy, making her increasingly uncomfortable with the wild intensity of his gaze. She was beginning to wonder if hypnosis was one of his tricks. When the phone rang next to him and he took his eyes off her, she let out a sigh of relief and relaxed slightly.

"Howling Mad Murdock here," he blathered into the mouthpiece. "I've got the time if you've got the beer."

"Hey, Murdock. Lynch just fell onto us. He may be heading your way." It was Hannibal. "He may get real tough."

Murdock cupped his hand over the phone and told Amy, "Excuse me, but I gotta be alone with my phone. . . ."

Amy nodded and backpedaled to the door, letting herself out into the hallway. Murdock waited until she had closed the door behind her, then put the phone back to his face.

"What's going on there, Murdock?" Hannibal asked him. "You making porno ink blots again?"

"Hannibal, I got some company standing in the hall right now . . ."

"Lynch? Is he there already?"

"No," Murdock whispered, sounding completely sane. "A girl reporter. She knows I flew you guys in Nam . . . got a whiff of Pentagon records or something, must be . . ."

"A reporter?"

"Yeah." Murdock had exercised his ration of normality for the day. A Mexican accent crept into his voice now, making him sound like the Frito Bandito. "Only she say she gotta job for us, mon. . . . Mehico. Olé, la bama! We search for a missing señor . . . *La Grande Siesta* with Señorita Lauren Bacall and—"

"Murdock, Murdock, turn it off a second, okay?" On the line Murdock could hear Hannibal groaning to himself before going on. "Look, be careful of the reporter. If it looks legit, send her to the alley behind the Kozy Kat Klub at two tonight. And be careful of Lynch. Okay?"

Picking a foam rubber football off his bed, Murdock drew the phone cord taut as he wandered across the linoleum to the fiber glass backboard hanging from the wall a few feet lower than regulation height. "Don't worry about

Colonel Geek. I'll slam-dunk that li'l sucker.'' Murdock demonstrated his intention by reaching up and forcing the foam ball through the hoop, then underwent still another transformation, physically shriveling as he spouted, in his finest Gibranese, ''And may the Great Spirit watch over your refrigerator and keep it cold . . . world without end, adios.''

Murdock hung up on Hannibal and leaned across the brass headboard of his bed, pulling the door open for Amy and gesturing her in as he plopped down on the mattress.

''Sorry,'' he apologized. ''That was my mother on the phone.''

Amy smirked as she reentered the room, telling Murdock, ''Funny, the file I got on you said your mother passed away when you were five years old.''

''She did,'' Murdock confessed, leaning back against the headboard and putting his hands behind his head. ''But I . . . I had a line put in . . . y'know . . . what a hassle, I'm tellin' ya. The telephone company doesn't cooperate like they used to. Took a while, but now we're solid.'' Murdock brought his hands around and clasped them together to emphasis the supposed newfound solidarity between himself and Ma Bell.

Amy pried open her clipboard and flashed Murdock a glimpse of the files she'd gotten from Bill Zachary earlier in the day. ''So you never heard of the A-Team?'' she said dubiously, exposing the glossies of the men in question. ''Of any of these guys?''

''Look, I got problems, y'know?'' Murdock snapped, springing from his bed and moving back over to the sink, where he began to spray random gobs of shaving cream onto his hair.

''What?'' Amy stared at Murdock with disbelief as he

reached for a twin-track razor and hoisted it above his head. "Murdock, what are you doing?"

"I'm shaving," Murdock responded matter-of-factly, glancing over his shoulder at Amy while keeping the razor in hovering position overhead. "Come on, ain't you ever seen a guy shave in the morning?"

Amy watched him turn back to the mirror, deciding that she was wasting her time here. "Look, I'm sorry for what happened to you," she said on her way to the door. "I'll see you around, Murdock . . ."

Murdock bolted from the sink and intercepted Amy before she could leave. "The A-Team?" he asked her. "Go to the alley behind the Kozy Kat Klub in Hollywood at two A.M. Wait for someone to contact you."

"For sure?" Amy asked, still skeptical.

Murdock fluttered his eyelids and bounced on the balls of his feet as he assured her, "Like, toooooootally."

SIX

Just as Amy rounded one end of the hallway and departed from the hospital, Colonel Lynch made his way down the other, flanked by the same nurse who had led the reporter to Murdock's room. Lynch was striding briskly, a figure of cocksure determination. He'd had a chance to change uniforms after the aborted chase at Universal Studios, but with each step he was reminded of the indignity heaped on him by Hannibal Smith, as a small pocket of trapped water sloshed dully against his inner ear with aggravating persistence.

As they closed in on Murdock's room, Lynch said, "I've got a hunch this guy isn't anywhere near as crazy as he pretends to be."

"He's not faking," the nurse insisted. "Mr. Murdock has paranoid anxiety delusions and intermittent memory loss. This week's specials. Next week he's due for another bout of schizophrenia. He's a regular Baskin case."

"You mean basket case, don't you, Nurse?" Lynch inquired.

The nurse shook her head. "Baskin, as in Baskin-

Robbins. Thirty-one flavors of mental illness. Murdock serves them all up sooner or later.''

"I see," Lynch said. "Well, I'm still gonna press him hard . . . see what happens. That won't snap him, will it?"

They stopped before the door, and the nurse told Lynch, "No. He's usually lots of fun. However, if he starts talking about ammonia, that's a clue he may become violent."

Lynch smiled blandly, and his Adam's apple bobbed nervously up and down inside his throat. "Violent?"

"It almost never happens, but just watch out," the nurse advised, turning the door handle. "It's a trigger word for his aggressive cycle."

"I'll keep that in mind, Nurse."

Forewarned, Lynch stepped past the nurse and entered the room, ready for anything. He found Murdock pacing frantically about the room, glancing under furniture, one arm held out stiffly before him as if it were holding onto a runaway lawnmower.

"Ho, Billy," Murdock was calling out, paying no mind to his visitors as he continued searching the room. "C'mon, Billy, where you hidin' now?" His gaze wandered up and locked briefly on Lynch and the nurse, betraying no sign of recognition. "You seen my dog Billy?" he asked them.

Colonel Lynch shook his head patiently, and the nurse smiled ingratiatingly as she did the same. Murdock continued to spin around the room, then, carried by his own momentum, he suddenly sprang up onto the top of a nearby cabinet and sat down, pulling his legs up and in so that he stared down at Lynch over the top of his kneecaps. A loony smile curved across his face as he called out, "Hi, Colonel. Bring any candy?"

The nurse came up alongside Lynch, injecting authority into her voice as she addressed the resident madman. "Mr. Murdock, get down from there!"

"From where?" Murdock asked, confused.

"Off the cabinet."

"Don't worry, leave him up there," Lynch said calmly, offering the nurse a conspiratorial wink. "Doesn't bother me. I'll take it from here."

"Are you sure?" the nurse asked.

Lynch nodded and waited for her to leave the room before turning his attention back to Murdock, who remained perched atop the cabinet. "And who are we today?" Lynch asked, his voice dripping with sarcasm. "Harold Lloyd? King Kong? Napoleon's parrot?"

"You think that's funny?" Murdock complained. "I'm not nuts. I keep telling everybody. Don't you think I wanna get outta here and see *E.T.*, just like everybody else?"

"I have this sneaking feeling you're faking, Murdock," Lynch maintained.

"If you could prove that, I'd sure appreciate it," Murdock said, squirming like a jack-in-the-box about to pop. "See, they think I'm a loony tunes. I keep . . . I was just saying . . ." His eyes suddenly rolled upward, and his head began to bob and jerk as if it were resting on a loose spring. The spasms spread throughout his body, and he hopped about the top of the cabinet, spouting off a torrent of multilingual gibberish, like someone with a hot line to the Holy Ghost.

Unperturbed by this demonstration, Lynch waited for

Murdock's fit to subside, then told him, "You flew the A-Team's mission over the DMZ. You were their pilot all through Nam. You dropped off Smith, Baracus, and Peck when they did their Hanoi bank jobs. And I think you're still working for them."

Murdock threw up his hands and briefly flapped his arms. "Hey, Colonel, if you say I flew 'em, then by cracky I flew 'em." He relaxed a moment, seemingly relieved by Lynch's accusations. "It's sure good to have at least one fact straight. Y'know? I mean, with everything so vague these days . . ." His eyes clouded suddenly, and his chin swung up so that he was looking at the ceiling. "What were we talking about?"

Lynch had had enough. He stared angrily at Murdock and boomed, "I'm not going for this. No way, Soldier. I'm not going for it."

"Neither am I," Murdock shot back.

"Good," Lynch said, taking a step forward. "Now that—"

"Hey, watch out!" Murdock suddenly wailed, staring bug-eyed at Lynch's feet. "Watch out!"

Lynch froze and looked down at his shoes, then back up at Murdock. "What now, Soldier?"

"Ammonia," Murdock whimpered pathetically, pulling himself into a ball as he stared with horror at the gleaming linoleum. His voice was choked as he spoke. "They use it on the floors. It eats through the soles of your shoes. Burns your feet."

"What?"

"Why d'ya think I'm sitting on top of this cabinet?" Murdock cried. "I'm not up here for the fresh air!"

Lynch stayed where he was, scrutinizing the hunched

figure before him. Murdock was shaking in place, and beads of sweat were beginning to form along the pale expanse of his brow, which was contorted into deep furrows that gave him the look of someone who'd come too close to the edge. The colonel was having second thoughts about his initial suspicions concerning Murdock's condition. Also, for the first time he noticed the bald spots pocking the inmate's scalp.

"What happened to your head, Murdock?"

Murdock frowned as if he didn't understand the question, then reached up, feeling for the spots he'd shaved moments before Lynch had arrived. Sobbing morosely, he explained, "Th . . . they hook you up to this . . . this machine, and then . . . then they give ya a zaperoo . . . right in the ol' noggin."

"You're in electric shock therapy?"

"I know that," Murdock said, his mood now swinging from depression to anger. "That's why I got these little shaved spots. They slap all this juice into me and . . ." Murdock leaned forward and sniffed the air like a bloodhound onto a fresh scent. He became increasingly agitated. "Can you smell it?" he howled adamantly. "Damn ammonia on everything! I hate ammonia. Hate everything! Hate my dresser. Hate my straitjacket. Man, I hate *you*!"

Murdock pointed a spindly finger at Lynch, who backed away, reaching behind himself for the doorknob. The colonel didn't like the psychotic sparks dancing in Murdock's eyes. "I'm sorry I troubled you, Soldier," he apologized, opening the door and backing out into the hallway. "Take care of yourself."

Murdock suddenly went airborne, springing forth from atop the cabinet and landing on all fours in his bed.

Lynch cleared the doorway and hurriedly closed the door behind him. Left alone, Murdock tilted his head back and let out a yelp like a coyote on a lonely night.

Colonel Lynch's aide, an officious-looking young man suited up in full military uniform, was waiting in the hallway. He looked worriedly at his commanding officer, then fell in step beside Lynch as the colonel headed down the hall, shaking his head to himself.

"You ought to see his record," Lynch muttered sadly. "Flew everything from jets to choppers. Hell, he was in the Thunderbirds before the war. One of the best combat pilots in Nam."

"And now . . . ?" the aide asked as they turned the corner and headed down the steps leading from the building.

"He's snapped," Lynch said. "No doubt about it."

"Too bad." The aide held the door open for Lynch, then followed him outside. Clouds were moving in from the coast, throwing their shadows across the grounds of the hospital. "I thought he was going to be able to help us out."

As they approached the parking lot, passing a pair of Korean War vets walking trancelike across the lawn, Lynch said, "We still have one lead to go on . . . that girl who called here trying to get a line on Hannibal Smith." The mere mention of his nemesis's name angered the colonel, and he tilted his head to one side and banged it lightly with the heel of his palm. To his surprise, the water trapped inside his head was dislodged by the blow and rolled wetly out his ear.

The aide pretended not to notice Lynch's strange action and moved to the passenger side of the limousine.

As he opened the door for the colonel, the aide said, "Amy Allen's her name. Newspaper lady. I think she was just hunting up a story. Like that guy last year."

"Maybe," Lynch said, getting into the car. "But stake her out. It's the only lead we've got left now. I want to know where she is every minute."

SEVEN

The Kozy Kat Klub hugged the corner along one of the seamier stretches of Sunset Boulevard, across the street from a walk-up hotel that rented most of its rooms by the hour. The Klub's exterior was adorned with a coat of paint that had been a garish shade of electric pink years ago but had since faded to the color of anemic flesh. Seething bulbs of incandescent light flickered around the frame of a sign promising the best in exotic titillation to the pruriently inclined. A nearby bank clock was flashing the time as 1:45 when Amy eased her Cutlass into a parking place down the block and stepped out into the downpour that had been bombarding the city for most of the night. Hunching over, she pulled up the collar of her trench coat and tugged it over her head to keep most of the rain from her hair.

"This better be worth it," she grumbled under her breath as she sidestepped the islands of trash littering the puddled sidewalk. Drawing close to the entrance, she spied another sign posted on the door, advising that one had to be over twenty-one and unoffended by the prospects of topless entertainment to enter the premises. Amy passed the first criterion, but if it weren't for the fact that she was seeking out the A-Team, the only way she'd come near the Kozy Kat Klub would be with a placard to hold in a picket line.

She was still staring at the recessed entrance when the door suddenly burst open, releasing the rhythmic strains of some obscure disco song that lent itself to the removal of clothing while dancing. Two men tumbled out as well, swaggering drunkenly forward and leaning on one another like a two-headed freak with four front feet. Amy recoiled from their advance, but not quickly enough to step clear of their lurid glances.

"Hey hey," one of the men cackled above the dive-bomber whistle of his companion. "Whadda we got here? You the new dish they're servin' up inside?"

"Yum yum," drooled the other man. "I thought I'd had my fill already, but suddenly I'm hungry again. Uuuummmmmm, boy . . ."

Amy quickly glanced up and down the street, but the only other person out braving the rain was a vagrant trying desperately to make room for himself inside the shopping cart that served as his mobile home.

"How about we pop across the street, chickiepoo?" the heftier of the two men asked as he and his partner broke their embrace and moved out so that they could close in on Amy from both sides, cutting off her avenue of escape. Behind them the door to the Klub slammed shut. Amy sensed from the looks in the men's eyes that their brains had taken the night off and left their glands to do the thinking for them. They seemed intent only in having their way with her.

"No thanks," she said tactfully, taking a step back toward the curb.

"Hey, come on," the thin man whined. "Look, let's be democratic here." He winked as his cohort, then proposed, "All those in favor of a quick date, say 'aye.' "

"Aye!" the hefty man said, blinking the rain from his eyes.

"Aye!" the thin man said, raising his hand at his side.

"Aye!" Amy said, matching the men's lascivious smile with one of her own, although she took care to dab a forefinger at her upper lip as if she were trying to hide something. "Of course, I have a slight case of herpes, but it's nothing to worry too much about."

"Say what?" the thin man said, frowning.

"Hey, come on, boys," Amy laughed cheerfully, taking another step toward the curb and gesturing over her shoulder at the hotel across the street. "Let's go get out of the rain and have some fun, okay?"

The two men looked at one another, sobering by the second. The hefty man finally shrugged his shoulders and headed away from Amy, muttering, "Come to think of it, Al, I'm kinda beat."

"Yeah, me, too, Hank. Mebbe we oughta move on and catch ourselves some zees, huh? Don't wanna be hung over for the ball game."

"Damn straight, Al." The hefty man shook his head at Amy and said, "Sorry, sweetstuff."

"How about a rain check?" Amy asked, trying to sound disappointed.

"I don't think so," Al murmured, falling into step next to Hank as they beat a quick path through the downpour to a pickup truck parked in front of Amy's Cutlass.

To be safe, Amy stepped into the entranceway to the Klub and waited until the pickup's engine sputtered into life and carried her would-be tormentors off down Sunset toward the nearest freeway exit that would take them back to their tract homes in the suburbs and wives who would give them hell for not having more sense than to come home out of the rain. After the anxiety of the ordeal she'd just been through, there was no way Amy was going to go inside the Klub and deal with more men fuelled by some stripper's last dance of the night. As soon as the rain subsided to a steady drizzle, she left the front of the building and trembled uncertainly as she braved the side alley leading to the back. There were two rear entrances, and patrons were heading out one of them and making their way to cars choking the cramped parking area. Amy took refuge in the second doorway, which was flanked on either side by a garbage dumpster and stacked cardboard boxes that were slowly collapsing under the weight of the rain. Through the door she could hear a pulsating bass line and rowdy yawps from men nursing two-dollar beers. Several minutes passed and the jukebox shut down, much to the disenchantment of the crowd. A booming male voice told the men to finish their beers and take a hike, since there wasn't going to be an encore.

By 2:30 the Kozy Kat Klub had been vacated, and still no one had arrived to make contact with Amy. The rain had picked up again, and the dripping from the eaves above the doorway was driving her mad.

"Why did I listen to that lunatic Murdock?" Amy whispered bitterly. "What kind of a reporter takes tips from a nuthouse? This is ridiculous. Al Massey's probably trapped in some prison and I'm wasting my time here in—"

" 'Raaaaaaindwopsss kip foolin' with my head,' " a wine-soaked voice sang out somewhere in the darkness. " 'But dat dozn't mean my eyes will havta go to bed . . .' "

"Hello?" Amy called out nervously, leaning forward and squinting her eyes as she peered through the downpour, spotting a hulking form wobbling alongside the dumpster toward her, now humming to himself as he waited for the next verse to come to him.

The man was wearing a sheet of plastic like a shawl, and the rain pattered noisily off him as he walked, pausing every few steps to take sustenance from a bottle concealed inside the soggy skin of a brown paper bag. From his looks it was clear that the bottle was getting the better of him. An ungroomed beard roamed freely across his face like a gray fungus, and his eyes fogged in and out of focus with every blink.

Amy wasn't sure what to do. The man had come up on her so suddenly that she found herself boxed in by him as he wavered before the doorway and looked up at her. He hiccuped and lost his tenuous grip on the bottle. It slipped from his fingers and landed with an explosive crash on the asphalt. The man looked down at the scattered shards and seemed on the verge of tears.

"My . . . my last bottle," he moaned pathetically.

"Are you okay?" Amy asked him, letting down her guard slightly but still keeping her hands clasped tightly around the straps of her purse, which was weighted down with a cassette recorder and enough other paraphernalia to pack the wallop of a blackjack if the need arose. "It's raining. You'll catch cold."

The wino tilted his head to one side and regarded Amy a moment before responding, "If I answer no questions, I tell no lies."

"Don't you have someplace you can go?" Amy said. "Where do you live?"

"In a box," the man sighed, beginning to shuffle away from Amy. "In the alley."

"Wait, wait," Amy said, abandoning the dryness of the doorway to catch up with the wino. He slowed his step and slowly turned to her. Amy quickly rifled through her purse and came up with a few stray bills. "Here," she insisted, jamming the currency into the man's grimy hand. "Take it. Buy some food, or something. Please."

The man's fingers closed around the money, and he pulled his hand inside the sleeve of his coat like the head of a turtle retreating inside its shell. He offered Amy a weak smile and crooned "You are a princess in a world of dragons."

As the man stumbled off into the night, Amy fought back an urge to follow him, not wanting to miss out on the chance, however slim it now seemed to be, that her liaison with the A-Team could be instigated as promised by Howling Mad Murdock. Had she followed the wino, she would have learned that the anticipated contact had already been made, because once the man had rounded the building, his stride widened and he reached into his pockets for a set of keys, one of which fit snugly into the passenger's door of a Ford LTD parked at the corner. Tossing aside the plastic sheet, he got into the car and let out a sigh of satisfaction as he began clawing at the artificial growth on his face. Once he was himself again, Hannibal Smith took his first close look at the money Amy had given him. To his surprise, he found himself holding a pair of twenties.

"I like your style, Miss Allen," he said with a smile, staring out through the windshield at the rain. "Now, if you can pass the Mr. Lee test, you've hired the A-Team. . . ."

EIGHT

Mr. Lee showed up the following morning, thumping his fist on the hood of Amy's Cutlass. She was stretched out across the front seat, fast asleep until the pounding noise wrenched her to consciousness. Disoriented, she jerked upright, her heart slamming hard against her chest, fuelled by a sudden blast of adrenaline. Once she'd managed to blink the sleep from her eyes, she winced at the pain seeping through her skull, aggravated by the pounding of the mean-faced Oriental who railed at her from the curb.

"Hey, missy . . . hey, missy!" Mr. Lee screeched, "You no park. Peoples coming . . . no park . . . you must leave!"

"Huh? What . . . ?" Amy said, pressing fingers against her throbbing temples.

"No park!" Mr. Lee said, pointing to the curbside sign backing him up. "Law say no park. You go. You go."

"Please," Amy pleaded as she rolled down her window. "You don't have to yell at people."

"Yellow people?!" Mr. Lee raged, shaking with so much anger his black-rimmed glasses threatened to slip from his face. "Yellow people! You no like yellow people?"

"No, not yellow people," Amy corrected. "Yell *at* people. Don't yell at me, okay? I've got a terrible headache."

"You got headache! I got laundry!" Mr. Lee jabbed a finger at the storefront behind him. The sign over the entrance bore his name and boasted laundry as his specialty. "People no park here. You go."

"Okay, okay," Amy sighed, realizing the futility of further conversation. "I'll move it. What time is it?"

"Seven and half," Mr. Lee told her. "Open early. People come before work. One-day service. Fold and fluff, only a buck."

Amy nodded feebly and raised a hand to quiet her tormentor before asking him, "You wouldn't happen to have an aspirin, would you? I'll buy it from you."

Mr. Lee eyed her sternly, stroking the black bristle of his goatee. His face slowly softened, and he finally reached down and opened her door. "You come," he said. "I fix."

"What about the car?"

As he helped her out of the Cutlass, Mr. Lee philosophized, "The Master say: 'Only the very wisest and the very stupidest cannot change.' "

"Confucius?" Amy groaned, standing upright and feeling her muscles cringe with stiffness. "Great. That's just what I need right now."

The skies had spent their fury, and only a handful of ragtag clouds remained perched above the city. The morning sun was beating down warmly, drying the sidewalks and throwing long shadows across the street. This part of town seemed less threatening than it had the night before, but Amy was still anxious to leave it behind. The failed rendezvous with the A-Team still weighed bitterly on her mind, and as she followed Mr. Lee into the Laundromat, she tried to plot another course of action. All normal channels had been exhausted, but she thought that if she just went down to Mexico on her own and hoped for the best, she might be able to stumble onto something or someone that would help her find Al Massey. It was a bleak prospect, but at this stage it seemed to be the only option remaining for her.

The Laundromat was fragrant with the scent of starch and detergent, and the walls vibrated slightly with the rumble of hot water coursing through old pipes on their way to the army of washing machines warming up in the back room. Mr. Lee left Amy at the front counter and vanished a few moments behind the faded curtain separating the shop front from the rear quarters, then returned with a cup of steaming green tea and two aspirin.

"Here," he said, setting the tea on the counter and handing Amy the aspirin. His demeanor had softened somewhat, and he watched her with concern as she swallowed the pills and sipped tea to wash them down.

"Thank you," she said, taking some change from her rumpled trench coat and placing it on the counter next to the tea saucer. "I appreciate it."

Amy was turning to leave when Mr. Lee called out, "You look for A-Team?"

Amy whirled about and stared at Mr. Lee. "How did you know about that?"

"Many Chinese in Viet Nam," Mr. Lee said cryptically. "Many people know A-Team. Very, very expensive. Very, very good."

As she headed back to the counter, Amy's face flushed with newfound hope. She began to explain, "A friend of mine disappeared. Al Massey. He's a reporter for the—"

"A-Team know," Mr. Lee cut her off. Before Amy could say anything more, he went on, "How much money missy got?"

The question took her by surprise, but only for a moment. She remembered the file on the A-Team and quickly realized that they weren't called soldiers of fortune without reason. "I have a house, and I have some stocks and bonds." Mr. Lee was nodding his head in such a way to indicate he was looking for a more specific figure. "I could raise maybe a hundred and fifty thousand dollars."

Mr. Lee pursed his lips and gave his head a brief shake. "No is enough. A-Team cost more."

"More?" Amy gasped. "Who do these guys think they are? More than that? Are you kidding?"

"Man with goatee not necessarily have kid," Mr. Lee said. Noting the perplexed expression on Amy's face, he explained, "Kid is baby goat. Just a small joke."

"Wonderful," Amy said dryly. "Look, Mr. Lee, I'm not going to put out that kind of money for a comedy act."

Mr. Lee sighed patiently, inspecting his fingernails. "The Master say: 'Women and people of low birth are hard to deal with.' "

"I can't wait to pass that along," Amy said.

In the back room, one of the washers rattled loudly as it changed cycles. Mr. Lee moved aside the empty teacup and leaned across the counter, lowering his voice dramatically. "How much is life worth today? Market change. In Viet Nam life cheap. Here, price high. How much Al Massey life is worth?"

"Everything I own," Amy responded without hesitation. "He's been like a father to me. He got me my first job and—"

"You get money," Mr. Lee interrupted. "Bring Al

Massey picture. If no hear from me in two days, is no deal. Good-bye, missy.''

''But, Mr. Lee—''

''The Master say: 'When the small man goes wrong, it is always on the side of elaboration.' Good-bye.''

''What?''

With a terse bow Mr. Lee turned from Amy and shuffled off to the back room. She watched the curtain close behind him and waited until it hung still in the doorway before leaving the Laundromat, shaking her head to herself. ''You're a real trip to the zoo, Mr. Lee,'' she sighed.

Back in the laundry room, Mr. Lee peered out through a slit in the curtain. Once he saw that Amy had left, he grinned widely, exposing bright white teeth, too perfect to be true. Grabbing hold of his bicuspids, Mr. Lee yanked out the whole set of teeth, revealing a smile that was a shade yellower but no less filled .with satisfaction. The goatee went next, and Hannibal Smith rubbed the chin that had become tender from the continued application of false hairs the past few hours. After shedding his glasses and black wig, he flicked off the lights and moved through the shadows to the front door, where he took time to reset the burglar alarm before exiting from the building. Outside, he withdrew a small locksmith's kit from his pocket and fidgeted with the front lock. The tumblers resisted at first, then cooperated and released the dead bolt into the metallic embrace of the strike plate assembly. He was putting the kit back in his pocket when a loud voice boomed out behind him.

''Hey, mac, we're not open yet!''

Hannibal turned around to face a tall, beefy Irishman wearing a pale blue uniform. A patch over one pocket read ''LEE'S LAUNDRY.'' The man's name was stitched in cursive lettering over the other pocket. His name was Lee Bowman.

"Oh, sorry," Hannibal apologized.

"Just give me a few minutes," Bowman said, fitting a key into the lock and opening the door. "I've got a couple cycles going. They'll be done by eight thirty. Are you Mr. Rembo?"

"Afraid not," Hannibal said. "I'll just stop by later."

"Suit yourself."

As Bowman went into his building, Hannibal headed off down the street and ducked into a greasy spoon advertising the best hashed-browns in L.A. He had some eating to do, and some planning, too.

The A-Team was in business.

NINE

St. Bartholomew's Convalescent Hospital was an austere brownstone building huddled on a shrub-choked knoll overlooking what had once been a rolling orchard filled with the aroma of orange blossoms and ripening citrus. Times had changed, though, and now the hospital's east wing afforded a view of newly built designer homes set on two-acre parcels of land linked by horse trails and an asphalt path allowing a private security force to patrol the estates on glorified golf carts. For years Monsignor David Magill had presided over the chapel at St. Bartholomew's concurrently with his duties as administrative head of the Sacred Heart Orphanage, located a mile's walk from the hospital. The monsignor had kept himself in good shape by making daily treks between the two establishments, but age had caught up with him, bringing with it a respiratory ailment that now confined him to a ground-floor room at the hospital, where he was tended to by a parade of caring nurses while he devoted himself to the appreciation of beauty in the hearts of good men and other thoughts that brought him joy. One of those good men who brought a special warmth to the monsignor's soul was Templeton Peck, the Face Man.

It was early in the afternoon when the door to the monsignor's room creaked open and Peck entered, offering his aged mentor a smile filled with a lifetime of hard-earned admiration.

"Still loafing, I see," Face Man said and smirked as he drifted over to the window, adjusting the shades and then toying with the dial of a small portable radio set on the commode next to the monsignor's bed.

"You're late, my boy," Magill crooned in a voice still simmering with a feisty Irish brogue. "I was wondering if you forgot."

"Not a chance, and you know it."

"Come closer," the monsignor beckoned, straining forward in his bed and curling a withered finger at the Face Man. "I can't see ya, boy. My peepers aren't what they once were."

"Okay." Face Man grabbed hold of a chair and swung it over alongside the bed, then leaned over the old man before sitting down. He kept one hand fluttering about his throat, but the monsignor quickly picked out what the younger man was trying to hide.

"What is that you're wearin', lad? Is it a clerical collar?" The monsignor squinted a few moments, then reached to his pocket for the assistance of his bifocals. As he had suspected, he found that the Face Man was wearing a black shirt and a short-trimmed collar over the white, starched band of a priest. The monsignor clucked his tongue as he removed the glasses and shook his head with mock gravity. "When will ya stop it, son?"

"Monsignor . . ." Face Man said, adjusting the collar slightly so that he could breathe easier. "Look, they won't let hardly anyone in to see ya except doctors and family. I figured that even a monsignor needs spiritual guidance in his hour of need . . . you know, a confessor of—"

"And so ya run off an' ya steal a clerical collar," the monsignor groaned. "My boy, the devil is hoverin' over ya like a vulture over a dyin' carcass, sure as I'm lyin' here. . . ."

"No, he's not, Monsignor," Face Man insisted, taking the older man's hand and giving it an affectionate squeeze. "You wouldn't let him."

Magill let out a surprisingly robust laugh and a tinge of color rose to his cheeks. He returned the squeeze, expending the limits of his strength, then let out a sigh and sank back against the pillows propped up against his headboard. "Well, I suppose I wouldn't. You've been quite a project in my life, son. Ever since you wandered in off the streets . . . five years old, no home, no folks . . ." Memories swelled up in the old man's mind, and he smiled wistfully at their presence. A twinkle ignited in his pale blue eyes as he looked at Peck. "My, but you did keep all us old goats at the orphanage on our toes, you did. . . ."

"Well, you guys needed a challenge." Face Man chuckled. "You were falling asleep at the joint. Too many choirboys."

The two of them shared a few moments of laughter, then fell silent, giving the room over to the final strains of a Mantovani arrangement pouring over the small speaker of the radio.

"I've been givin' ya a lot of thought, son," the monsignor finally resumed, adopting a serious tone. "I've been wondering what's gonna become of you when I'm not around to pray for your shenanigans."

"I'm doing okay," Face Man said, reaching into the

pocket of his coat and pulling out a portable card carrier the size of a cigar pack.

"Are ya now?" Magill sniffed. "First you're orphaned by your parents, and then your country. And now you spend every Saturday with me in here . . ."

"Listen, Monsignor," Face Man said, setting the card box next to the radio before turning his attention back to the ailing cleric. "Except for Hannibal, you're the only one who ever invested in me. You don't have to like it, tough guy, but I'm payin' ya back, just the same."

"You have to invest in yourself, lad," the monsignor said firmly. "You have a streak of compassion in you that nobody but me ever sees. You've been handed some bad breaks, but you've got to face your problems."

The Face Man had heard this sermon at least a dozen times a year since his return from Nam, and, as with all the times before, he listened with patient attentiveness. In the end, though, his direction remained unchanged, as did his response. "I wanna get back. I'm tired of running," he admitted. "I'd like to have a family, but you can't do that with the government on your tail. In the meantime, I'll settle for just surviving."

"A shame," Magill sighed. "It's truly a shame."

"I don't make the rules, Monsignor. I just do the best I can playing the hand that's dealt me."

"Ha, leave it to Templeton Peck to talk about life like a card game," the monsignor mused.

"Shhhhh, I gotta get down to business here." Face Man turned up the volume on the radio, rapidly twisting the dial until a female voice replaced the liquid gushings of a hundred violins.

"This is Dr. Toni Clark and you're listening to *Psychology*

Chat Back,'' the woman informed her listeners. "Our next caller is Carl from Covina . . .''

"Damn,'' Face Man muttered.

"Don't you mean 'darn,' son?'' the monsignor admonished.

"Yes. That's exactly what I mean,'' Face amended, taking the card box and beginning to sort through the filed cards within. Anyone unfamiliar with Templeton Peck's background might have looked in the room and thought they were seeing an eccentric priest who'd made a habit out of jotting down the neuroses of talk show callers, but any such deduction was far off target from reality. For starters, the Face Man knew that the man speaking to Toni Clark was not Carl from Covina, but rather Hannibal Smith. . . .

"How you doing?'' Dr. Clark was asking her caller.

"Well, I'd like to say I'm doing fine, Toni,'' came the pathetic voice of Carl from Covina. "But . . . well, things have been really strange for me this month. . . .''

"Tell me about it,'' the radio psychologist urged.

While the caller hesitated a moment, Peck quickly flipped through the cards in his hand, skimming past the likes of "Bill from Torrance'' and "Mike from Woodland Hills'' until he finally came upon one with a heading that read "Carl from Covina.'' Underneath the heading was the coded message Hannibal was delivering.

JET AIRPLANE: THREE THOUSAND MILE RANGE
Light Armament
Passport Visa: Mexico

"Mexico,'' Face Man read out loud. "He wants to go to Mexico.''

"Well, I moved back in with my younger sister, and she's been controlling my life just like she did when we were kids," Hannibal finally managed to whine over the radio.

"Client's a woman," Face Man deciphered. "A young one."

"A pretty one, too, I hope," the monsignor whispered from his bed, having resigned himself to the fact that Peck was going to go on being a member of the A-Team despite any lectures to the contrary.

"Me too," Peck said.

The Face Man wasn't the only one listening to the woes of Carl from Covina with secret understanding. Miles away from the cloistered serenity of St. Bartholomew's, B.A. Baracus was holding court with a handful of youngsters at the Watts King Memorial Day Care Center. He was showing the kids how to make a skateboard out of an old plank of wood and a dismantled roller skate while the radio played softly in the background.

"How old is your sister, Carl?" Dr. Toni Clark was asking.

"She's twenty-five, but she's always been very assertive and I . . ." There was a sputter of sniffles over the speaker, then Carl from Covina continued, "Well, I hate confrontations. . . ."

"Sure you do, Hannibal," B.A. sneered at the radio.

One of the kids, a wiry ten-year-old by the name of Floyd, scratched his billowing Afro with confusion, then asked B.A., "Who's Hannibal, man?"

"Don't you know about Hannibal?" B.A. said. "You're goin' to school . . . don't they teach ya about Hannibal and them elephants?"

Floyd shook his head and looked to his friends, who all shrugged their shoulders. "Not yet," Floyd told B.A. "He had elephants?"

B.A. nodded as he screwed one set of wheels into place on the board. "Hannibal was this Carthaginian commander, man," he explained. "Long time ago. He hated the Romans 'cause they conquered his people, so he attacked 'em by taking his army over the Alps into Italy. He used elephants to carry his equipment. Nobody thought you could take an army over the Alps, but he did. Caught the Romans nappin' and beat 'em up."

"Wow!" Floyd gasped.

"Far out!" another of the kids cried out.

A third youth clapped his hands and cheered, "Bitchin'!"

"Hey, watch your mouth!" B.A. scolded, flexing his biceps and eyebrows. "We don't have none of that toilet mouth stuff around here, got it?"

The young offender stared down at the ground shamefacedly, then stammered, "Hey, I'm sorry, man."

"Fair enough," B.A. said, giving the boy a light punch on the shoulder. "Just watch it."

The day care center was located adjacent to an industrial park, and when the loud groan of machinery started to emanate from the nearby buildings, B.A. leaned over and turned up the volume on the radio, just in time to hear Dr. Clark bringing her conversation with Carl from Covina into the advisory phase.

"It's your life, Carl," she informed her caller. "What do you think you should do?"

Carl from Covina thought it over a moment, then said, with newfound determination, "I got this friend who drives race cars. I was thinking maybe I'd call him and have him pick me up at three this afternoon so we can go to the races this weekend . . . not askin' my sister's permission or nothing!''

"I think that's a wonderful idea!" Dr. Clark gushed encouragingly.

B.A. snapped off the radio, then quickly drove home the last screw in the skateboard. He tested the play of the wheels against his massive palms before he handed the board to Floyd and rose to his feet, saying, "I gotta be goin'. Gotta pick up a friend at three o'clock.''

The kids all groaned in unison.

"Hey, man, stay awhile longer," Floyd begged. "Tell us some more about Hannibal.''

"Hannibal's one piece of work, I'll tell you that much," B.A. said with a grin, signaling over the kid's shoulder for the day care supervisor to take over for him.

"You make it sound like he's still alive," Floyd said.

"Yeah, how 'bout that." B.A. patted all his young admirers on the shoulders and told them, "Look, I may be gone a couple of days.''

There were more groans as the kids followed B.A. toward the gate leading to the street.

"Come on, you guys, I gotta make a livin', you know," B.A. complained. "I'll see ya next week. Don't go stealin' no hubcaps while I'm gone or I'm gonna be mad. You don't want me mad, do you?''

"No way, B.A.," Floyd said on behalf of his playmates.

"Good." B.A. paused at the gateway and pointed back toward the grounds of the day care center. "Now go get your butts back there and have a good time playin', hear? Everybody take turns with that skateboard, and I'll make another one next time I'm by.''

"Heck, now that you showed us, we can do it ourselves," Floyd boasted.

"Yeah!" the others joined in.

As they turned and ran off, Floyd shouted, "We'll make one for everyone, then take 'on some of them hills out at the end of the street. Man, we'll be just like Hannibal's army!"

"I get to be Hannibal!" one of the others yipped.

"No way!" Floyd said.

B.A. watched the kids begin to argue and shook his head mumbling to himself as he left the gounds.

"Only one Hannibal," he said, his voice edged with pride. "World couldn't take more than one like that sucker."

TEN

The Face Man's assignment was to get Howling Mad Murdock out of the hospital and to secure a medium-range jet by three o'clock. He remembered watching episodes of *Mission: Impossible* back in the sixties, where they had a crew of at least six on hand to tackle less improbable tasks.

"Never make it easy if you can help it, do you, Hannibal," he mumbled to himself as he wheeled out of the driveway of a lavish Bel-Air mansion in a Cadillac Eldorado convertible with steer horns mounted over the engine as a hood ornament. Securing the car had taken charm, guile, fast talk, and more than a few of the prayers Monsignor Magill had promised to be saying nonstop for the duration of the A-Team's latest dance with danger. As he guided the monstrous automobile down the most scenic stretch of Sunset and across the San Diego Freeway, Peck patted down the lapels of his Marine jacket. The uniform was just one of many he'd appropriated from film lots during his few flings as a studio gofer over the years. As situations called for it, he could also impersonate ranking officers in the Army, Air Force, Navy, Coast Guard, and

Boy Scouts of America. Hannibal Smith, it seemed, hadn't cornered the market on false identities when it came to the A-Team.

En route to the Veterans' Administration Hospital, the Face Man tried out a few accents and speech patterns, finally deciding to go with a stern, authoritarian voice that reminded him of his first drill sergeant at boot camp back in the days before Nam. Entering the parking lot, he eased the Cadillac into a spot far from view of the main lobby of the hospital, then eyed himself in the rearview mirror and toyed with the brim of his cap until it was cocked at the angle that suggested the right tone of smug self-assurance. Properly psyched up, he exited from the car and strode forcefully across the parking lot and up the walk leading to the lobby. On the way he winked at enough young nurses to give the impression he was afflicted with a facial tic. The false moustache tickling his nostrils furthered the illusion.

The lobby was fairly deserted and presided over by a petite nurse sitting on a raised chair behind the information counter. When the Face Man entered, she glanced up at him momentarily, then turned her attention back to the letter she was writing back home to her mother. It wasn't until Peck loomed to a halt before her and clicked his heels with the snap of a salute that she looked back up at him.

"Lieutenant Blackman here to check out Captain Murdock for psychiatric evaluation," he announced briskly.

"Captain Murdock . . ." The nurse looked over the various ledgers set out before her, running a polished red fingernail across the pages like a bloodhound trying to sniff out the name of the man Face had asked for. While she was engrossed in the search, Peck spotted the nameplate on the counter and found out the nurse's last name was Schneider.

"I'm sorry," Nurse Schneider finally said, "we don't have any orders to that effect, Lieutenant."

The Face Man let go with a facial tic that changed his expression from pleasant to perturbed. He sighed, letting gruffness creep into his voice. "His file was chosen specifically by General Fred White, Surgeon General of the Air Force. We want an update on this man. I've personally gone to a lot of trouble checking his Uncle Deke out of the Fairview Mental Hospital. He's under guard at the Sheraton until we bring over his nephew. We're going to try some stress confrontation therapy."

To back his bluff, the Face Man handed the nurse a letter of authorization he'd thrown together on official-looking stationery he'd acquired at the same time he'd scrounged up his uniform. Nurse Schneider scanned the letter briefly, then handed it back, saying, "Fine, but I'm afraid I don't understand. What's this with his uncle? Uncle who?"

"His Uncle Deke Murdock . . . the cleaning fluid salesman." Peck leaned across the counter, lowering his voice to a tone of confidentiality. "Certainly you're familiar with his ammonia fixation."

"Yes," Nurse Schneider said with a nod, letting down her guard. "He hates the stuff."

"No," Face corrected, indulging a smile upon the nurse. "He hates his Uncle Deke who used to sell ammonia. Classic hate transferal, Nurse Schneider."

"You're kidding!" The nurse unleashed a smile of her own, the kind that implied that she loved it when Peck talked like that.

The Face Man stood back from the counter, falling back to attention and his previous facade of officious impatience. "I find it's best not to kid about mental disorder . . . don't you, Nurse Schneider?" Satisfied that the display had brought the nurse back into line, he went on, "General White is personally interested in Captain Murdock because the captain flew him in Nam. I don't have a lot of time, Nurse. I only have his uncle out for the day because he's scheduled for a frontal lobe severance tomorrow."

"His uncle is having a lobotomy tomorrow?"

"The whole family is crackers," the Face Man confided. "How about it? Can we move this along? I don't have much time, and the general will be calling me at five."

As she picked up the office phone and dialed the exchange number for the psychiatric ward, Nurse Schneider told the Face Man, "We always wondered about that ammonia fixation and the aggressive cycle. A classic hate transferal . . . how fascinating!"

"Isn't it, though?" Peck said, smiling stiffly.

Nurse Schneider waited for an answer on the other line, then ordered, "Have Captain Murdock made ready for release. . . ." After she hung up, the Face Man exhausted his limited understanding of psychology trying to keep up a conversation with her without blowing his cover. By the time a hospital orderly was delivering Murdock to the lobby, Peck was into his third minute of improvisation about oedipal complexes.

"Ah, Captain Murdock, so good to see you again!" Peck said, sweeping away from the information counter toward his cohort. "You remember me, Lieutenant Blackman. The Surgeon General's assistant. Remember?"

"But I haven't smoked in years!" Murdock insisted.

"Well, of course if you count when they zap me, then I—"

"Now now, Captain, not to worry," the Face Man said calmly, taking Murdock by the arm and leading him away from the orderly. "We're just going to take you for a little ride; let you have a look at the world that's waiting out there for you once we've cured you."

"Oh yeah?" Murdock said hopefully. "Fantasy World? You mean we're going to Disneyland?"

"Well, not exactly . . ." Peck slipped Nurse Schneider a wink, then draped an arm across Murdock's shoulder as the two men headed out of the lobby into the warm afternoon. As soon as the door had closed behind them, he dropped his lieutenant act and looked around the grounds suspiciously. "Come on, Murdock, let's move it. Lynch could still be around here."

"Naw, I think I scared that mother off, but good," Murdock said with a grin as they took long strides down the walk. "Won't see him back here unless he's bringing a casting agent so I can try out for *Psycho III*. Tony Perkins, look out!"

"What did you do to your head?" the Face Man asked, noticing Murdock's pocked scalp. "You got lotsa little shaved spots up there."

"Yeah, I noticed those, too." Murdock said, touching the bald areas. "Crazy, huh?" As if to dispel any doubts about the matter, Murdock broke away from the path and chased a nurse across the lawn, howling, "Aw, you just gotta come to my hotel. You'll looooooove my mother!"

The Face Man hurriedly retrieved Murdock from the cluster of palm trees where he'd chased the frightened nurse. After apologizing to the woman, he led Murdock back to the parking lot, grumbling, "I think you're getting worse, pal."

"I know I am," Murdock admitted. "I'm surprised the Surgeon General let me out."

"He didn't, I did," the Face Man told him. "I had to bring your Uncle Deke into town."

"Ahhhhh," Murdock said, nodding his head knowingly. "How is ol' Uncle Deke, anyway?"

"You don't have an Uncle Deke."

Murdock shrugged his shoulders sadly as they approached the waiting Cadillac. "Sorry to hear it. I was just beginning to like him."

The Face Man circled around to the driver's side and unlocked the door. Opening it, he took off his cap and tossed it in the back seat, then started taking off his jacket as he told Murdock, "You hated him. He used to beat you."

"The creep." Murdock waited for Peck to unlock the passenger side, then climbed into the Cadillac and rubbed his hands over the leather interior and plush nap of the sheepskin seat covers. "Where'd you get this parade float?"

"Scrounged it from Cactus Jack Perkins, the rodeo rider," Face said, igniting the engine, then letting it warm up while he donned a ten-gallon cowboy hat adorned with a band of peacock plumes. "He thinks I'm doing a ring job on it over the weekend."

"That sounds like a job more up B.A.'s line," Murdock said, clamping the seat belt and shoulder harness across his body as the Face Man backed out of the parking lot and joined the traffic on San Vincente.

"Just a cover, my man," Peck said, starting to drawl like a Texan. "This here's our meal ticket to a nice new Gulf Stream. If I can get it, can you fly it?"

"Hey, brother, if it's got wings, I can fly it," Murdock boasted, beaming out the window at the passing storefronts. After they'd traveled a few blocks, he turned slowly to the Face Man and asked, "Hey, what's a Gulf Stream?"

ELEVEN

Amy Allen bypassed the elevator and took the back stairway up to her office at the *Courier-Express*. The only person to see her was Lorenzo Ghirl, an enigmatic widower of eighty whose primary pleasure in life was preparing the paper's daily obituaries and birth announcements. He'd performed the same minuscule task for the past fourteen years and had come to the point where he viewed himself as some form of intermediary deity, somewhat akin to the three fates. In his own way he felt that he had a say in the life-and-death matters of the city's populace, and as such he never felt obliged to concern himself with the more mundane doings of those around him. Amy Allen might have been no more than a clot of dust motes dancing in the afternoon sunlight for all the attention he paid to her as he entered the stairway on the seventh floor and walked past her on the way down to the paper's commissary.

Amy remained frozen in place until Lorenzo's footsteps ceased pattering on the concrete steps, then went to the door and let herself into the hallway. She figured she had a few minutes before people would start swarming back from their lunch breaks, so she hurried down the vacant corridor and slipped into her office. Going to her desk, she hurriedly went through her drawers, taking out the tools of her trade that she felt she would need for her upcoming "vacation." She opened up the attaché case she had brought along and filled it with pertinent files, travel brochures on Mexico, a microcassette recorder, three sets of long-life batteries, a dozen tapes, note pads, pencils, and a portable sharpener. Her nerves were on edge, and every time she heard a phone ring in one of the adjacent offices, a spurt of adrenaline zipped through her system, stirring up everything in its path. She knew that if her managing editor caught wind of her plans she wouldn't have a job to come back to.

At last she had everything packed, and by leaning on the upper half of the attaché case, she was able to snap the locks into place.

"Whew!" she exhaled, slinging her purse back over her shoulder and turning to head for the door. Before she could reach it, however, the door suddenly swung inward. Amy jumped back, letting out a frightened gasp.

"Hey, relax, it's just me," Bill Zachary said reassuringly, seeing her quake before him. "Easy."

"Thank God," Amy said once she'd caught her breath.

Zachary unbuttoned his sport coat and removed a wrapped parcel from the inner pocket. "I got the money . . . at least what I could manage to scrape up on such short notice."

Amy took the parcel and transferred it to her purse, telling her associate, "Thanks again, Zack. Like I told you on the phone, I'll give it right back if things fall through with the A-Team."

"No rush, Amy. I know you're good for it." Zachary backtracked and checked the hallway, then waved Amy out of the office and led her to the stairway. "If you can't get the A-Team, use the cash to do what you feel you have to. Just keep me posted, and don't do anything too foolish."

"Right." Once inside the stairway, Amy leaned over and gave Zachary a light kiss on the cheek as she squeezed his arm. "Wish me luck, Zack."

Zachary blushed and offered up a feeble grin. "I'll buy big shoes and keep my toes crossed."

Amy turned and bounded gingerly down the steps, reaching the basement without incident and exiting to the underground parking lot, a concrete cave shrouded from daylight and lined with cars resting under the fluorescent glow of overhead lamps. Her keys jangled loudly above the sound of her footsteps as she approached her Cutlass. She had just opened the rear trunk when a car lurched into life at the opposite end of the garage and raced toward her. It was the souped-up Rambler, and B.A. Baracus was behind the wheel. He braked to a halt alongside Amy as Hannibal Smith rolled down the back window and looked out at her.

"Amy Allen?" he asked in a way that indicated he already knew her identity. When Amy nodded her head numbly, still trying to bring her nerves under control, he went on, "I'm Hannibal Smith. I understand you want to hire the A-Team."

Amy's plan had been to drive back to Mr. Lee's Laundromat in hopes that he would arrange an introduction to the A-Team. To have half the group appearing before her with the unexpected suddenness of twin genies popping out of a bottle was too astounding for words. Her jaw quivered and her mouth gaped open, but nothing came out.

"What gives, woman?" B.A. snapped. "Can't you talk?"

"Uh . . . I . . . uhhh," Amy stammered.

"You got the picture of Massey and the money?" Hannibal asked patiently.

"Yes . . ."

"Okay," Hannibal said, reaching over the front seat and opening the passenger's door of the Rambler. "Let's go."

"What?" Amy finally managed to sputter.

"You want to go to Mexico?" Hannibal said.

"Yes, but . . . right this instant?" Amy said. "I'm not packed. What about my clothes? My car?"

"Lock it and leave it, Miss Allen," Hannibal told her. "You've got five seconds."

B.A. revved the Rambler's engine and glowered at Amy through the opened door. She hesitated for half the five seconds, then quickly slammed down the trunk hood of her Cutlass and got into the Rambler. B.A. had his foot on the accelerator before she was settled into her seat. She closed her door and held onto the armrest for dear life as the Rambler squealed around the corner and shot up the incline leading from the parking structure. A sunny California day was waiting for them as they hit the streets.

"Miss Amy Allen," Hannibal said once they were in traffic, "may I present Bosco Baracus . . . B.A."

"How do you do," Amy said, securing her seat belt before reaching across the stick shift to shake B.A.'s hand.

"Can't you see I'm drivin'?" B.A. barked, ignoring Amy's hand.

"Sorry," Amy said, already beginning to have her doubts about the company she was keeping.

"Don't worry," Hannibal called out from the back seat. "He's got a bad attitude, but he grows on ya!"

"How nice," Amy said, facing straight ahead, taking in

the scenery as if she wondered if she'd ever have a chance to see it again the way B.A. was driving.

If Amy or either of the two men had bothered to glance back, they might have noticed a dark sedan weaving through traffic trying to keep up with them. Behind the wheel was a man in a uniform holding before him a C.B. microphone through which he was informing Colonel Lynch that their surveillance of Amy Allen had put them back on the scent of the A-Team.

TWELVE

There was a second ten-gallon hat in the back seat of the Cadillac, and the Face Man reached for it with one hand as he used the other to jockey the car onto a private airfield lined with sleek, high-priced planes and minijets.

"Here you go, Murdock," he said, handing the hat to his partner. "Slap this on and start thinking cowboy. I've been laying the groundwork for this plane for almost two months. Just keep your mouth shut and let me handle things."

"Dad burn it, Mr. Favor, ya know ya kin count on me," Murdock drawled sarcastically as he angled the stetson on his head. His bald spots disappeared from view, and if it weren't for the fact that his ears propped up the hat, his whole face might have vanished as well. "Right comfy piece of headgear, boss. Doubles as a tepee in case I want ta hide out with the Injuns, right?"

As the svelte-looking saleslady bounded gaily out of the office they'd parked in front of, the Face Man put on a happy face and hissed out the side of his smile, "Put a zipper on it, Murdock. Avon here can't be disturbed while she eats outta my hand."

"Jo Bob Mathison," Avon oozed as she came up to the Cadillac, intercepting the Face Man on his way out of the driver's seat. "I didn't believe it when I saw your name on the message sheet. I thought you and your daddy Hank bought that Lear up in Santa Barbara."

"Howdy, Avon," Peck said, tipping the brim of his hat. "'Fore we start yammerin' away on these here business details, I'd like ya ta meet my personal pilot . . . fella by the name of Buster Hawthorn. Buster, give Avon a big howdy."

Murdock didn't seem too pleased with his alias. He smiled sourly at Avon and murmured, "Big howdy."

"Pleasure to meet you, Mr. Hawthorn," Avon said, offering Murdock a petite hand.

"Right," Murdock said, pumping her hand with his own. "Call me Bust for short."

"Say, Buster," Face interrupted, pointing to one of the nearby jets, "why don't y'all take a gander at that there Gulf Stream while me and Avon see if we're gonna be able ta cut us a calf here!"

"Sure thing, Jo Bob," Murdock replied, slipping his thumbs through his belt loops as he sauntered away from the Cadillac. Once he was beyond earshot of his cohort, he shook his head and grumbled, "And they call *me* nuts . . ."

The Face Man leaned against the front fender of his borrowed car, then crossed his arms to indicate that his preference was to discuss business outside rather than going into the office and having to peddle his scam to a wider audience. Avon had her clipboard with her and stayed put as well, figuring that by handling her client one-on-one she'd be assured a full commission on any sale.

"What happened to the Lear, Jo Bob?" she asked.

"Well, honey," Peck droned, "this here's gonna hand ya a big yahoo, but I got that little sucker home to Texas and Daddy Hank, he climbs aboard and he sits in the seat and damned if his stetson ain't brushin' the top of that cabin." He paused a moment and sighed, recalling the nonexistent memory. "Like t'drive Big Daddy Hank nuts, havin' that hat bangin' on the roof like that all the time."

"The Lear has a small cabin, all right," Avon said, "but he could just take his hat off and be rid of the problem, couldn't he?"

"Yep, yep, my thoughts exactly," the Face Man agreed, keeping a casual eye on Murdock, who was circling the Gulf Stream like a dog sniffing out a stranger. "But Big Daddy Hank don't never take off that there stetson on accounta he ain't got much grass growin' on the north end of his spread, if you know what I mean . . ."

"He's bald?" Avon guessed.

"As a dirt farmer's truck tire," the Face Man told her. "Like a new baby's butt, to put it another way."

"Jo Bob!" Avon twittered, pretending to be scandalized. Her smile gave her away, though.

"So he says t'me, 'Jo Bob' "—the Face Man widened his grin at Avon—"Daddy calls me Jo Bob, same as yourself . . . anyway, he says, 'Jo Bob, y'all go back ta L.A. an' get me that Gulf Stream you was talkin' about.' "

"Well, I'm certainly glad we still have the plane here," Avon said, easing into negotiating position. "I almost had a sale on it just a few days back, you know. That's a very popular set of wings."

The Face Man didn't respond to the bait. He let his gaze linger a moment on Murdock, who was now nosing around the cockpit of the jet, his face a picture of intense concentration.

"Jo Bob . . . ?"

"I was thinkin', y'know," Face finally said, polishing his knuckles on his chin. "Maybe if'n I could like test-fly that little sucker down t'Houston . . . Daddy Hank's down there tryin' t'horse-trade a few hotels and such. If I could sorta have Buster fly him around over the weekend, just make sure he ain't gonna have no problems with nothin' . . . hate t'have him knock his hat off in the john an' such . . . y'know?"

"I think that could be arranged," Avon said, taking a pen from her pocket and hovering it above the clipboard. "I'll have to make up a sales agreement, that's all . . ."

"Fantastic!" the Face Man enthused. He reached for his rear pocket like a moneyslinger about to draw his wallet. "Y'all want a little check or anything . . . a deposit of some sort?"

"I think your credit's okay with us, Jo Bob," Avon said.

"Now that's what I like to hear!" Peck said, pulling his hand away from his wallet and using it to pat Avon on the shoulder. "Then let's hog-tie the sucker . . ."

THIRTEEN

Like Achilles, B. A. Baracus's otherwise awesome being was subject to one specific weakness. He hated to fly. The mere thought of being airborne brought the muscle-bound mechanic fits of acute anxiety and paranoia. No one knew for sure the reasons for his phobia, and B. A. Baracus wasn't the sort of person to whom one readily recommended psychiatric care. Hannibal was fully aware of his companion's condition, though. As they drove across town, nearing the vicinity of the airfield where the Face Man was attempting to secure the Gulf Stream, he shifted his position in the back seat until he was partially hidden from B.A.'s range of vision in the rearview mirror, then discreetly unbuttoned the flap on his shirt pocket. Amy happened to glance back in time to see Hannibal remove a syringe from the pocket, along with a small glass bottle and a ball of cotton. Hannibal caught her eye and put a quick finger to his lips and motioned for her to look away from him.

As B.A. was whizzing into an intersection to beat a traffic light and negotiate a sharp left turn, Hannibal leaned forward slightly, dabbing the black man's exposed shoulder near the neck with the cotton ball. B.A. didn't pay much attention to the touch, but when Hannibal followed up by stinging him with the needle, he swatted at his shoulder with his free hand, almost slapping the syringe aside.

"What's goin' on, Hannibal?" B.A. growled, his senses suddenly alerted.

"Nothing, B.A.," Hannibal insisted, jerking the syringe and bottle out of sight. "Just take a right here, on this road."

B.A. made the turn, but quickly figured out what was happening. "Where we goin'?" He slowed the Rambler and rolled down the window, straining to catch the telltale sounds of planes in flight. There was noise in the wind, and it wasn't coming from birds. "I ain't goin' to no airport, Hannibal. I ain't gonna fly with that crazy fool Murdock."

"Murdock?" Hannibal said innocently. "Did I say Murdock?"

"Murdock?" Amy piped in with concern of her own.

"Yeah, man, that guy is nuts," B.A. complained. "If he's flyin', we're dyin'!"

"We're not going to the airport, B.A.," Hannibal insisted. "Now c'mon, take another right here."

B.A. took the corner wide, then slammed on the brakes as an ascending 747 roared above the surrounding rooftops and rattled the Rambler's framework with the forceful noise of its engines. Sweat beaded up on either side of B.A.'s Mohawk as he cringed in his seat, clutching tightly at the steering wheel. As the jet continued its ascent and the air around the car grew quieter, B.A. whirled around and told Hannibal, "Hey, sucker, that weren't no mosquito!"

"Okay, so we're going to a place *near* the airport," Hannibal confessed nonchalantly. "Big deal. Keep going and take another right."

"You just better not be jivin' me, Hannibal," B.A. warned, goading the car forward. He involuntarily reached to his neck and rubbed the spot where he'd been givin his injection of Novocaine. "Man, I just gotta smell an airplane and I get to feelin' bad."

"Hang in there, B.A., you're doing fine," Hannibal coached.

"I've met with Murdock," Amy said as B.A. followed Hannibal's directions. "Isn't he a little on the unstable side?"

"Lady," B.A. said, "they ain't got terms for what he is. Hey, Hannibal, I don't feel so hot."

The next turn took the Rambler through an untended gate and out onto a wide patch of asphalt lined with mounted lights. B.A. put two and two together and stopped the car again, this time turning off the engine. He threw open his door and climbed out, taking a good look in both directions before venting his rage on Hannibal. "We're at the airport, turkey! This here's a runway!"

"Where? Here?" Hannibal inquired as he got out on Amy's side of the car, after her, keeping the Rambler between himself and B.A. "Naw, this is just a taxiway *near* the runway."

B.A. bounded around the front of the Rambler, his eyes narrowing as they bored into Hannibal. Amy backed away from the pending confrontation, calling out, "What's going on? Will somebody please tell me?"

B.A. ignored Amy and took another step toward Hannibal. "You lied to me, man."

Taking a step back, Hannibal glanced quickly down at

his watch, then tried to fend B.A. off with a smile. "Lie? . . . Me?"

"I told you what I was gonna do next time you tried to take me on a plane ride. I told ya." From the way B.A. was flexing his muscles, it was clear that his earlier threats had something to do with violence.

"Please . . ." Amy begged, trying to figure out what was going on. "What's the meaning of this?"

Hannibal held his ground as the thick-muscled mechanic lumbered toward him. "Now, B.A., watch out," he advised. "If you don't watch it, you'll have another one of your anxiety blackouts."

B.A. pumped a right cross into Hannibal's face, sending him staggering backward until his balance gave way and he fell down. Hannibal quickly sat up, stroking his bruised jaw as he watched B.A. take another step toward him. "Come on, B.A., take it easy, will ya?"

B.A. suddenly stopped moving. He blinked several times, then collapsed at the knees and fell forward, sprawling out on the ground in front of Hannibal.

"I thought you were all on the same side," Amy said, rushing over to where Hannibal was getting back on his feet. "Why did he hit you?"

"Hit me?" Hannibal laughed. "Hell, if he had hit me, I'd be in the hospital. Come on, give me a hand with him."

B.A. was two hundred and thirty-five pounds of dead-weight, and it was with extreme difficulty that Hannibal and Amy dragged him back to the Rambler and stuffed him into the front passenger's seat.

"What was that shot you gave him, an elephant tranquilizer?" Amy said as she made sure B.A.'s legs were clear of the door before closing it.

"No, I ran out of those a few years back," Hannibal said. "I just gave him a little something from the sandman. B.A. travels so much better when he's well rested."

Amy climbed into the back seat as Hannibal got in behind the wheel and started up the Rambler. Just as he was putting the car into gear, he heard sirens cut through the din of the airfield. Looking around, he finally placed the sounds at another gateway at the opposite end of the runway, where three black sedans had poured out onto the runway and were righting their courses in the direction of the Rambler.

"How nice," Hannibal chuckled. "A bon voyage party to see us off. Hang on, Miss Allen. . . ."

The Rambler's tires raised a ruckus of their own as they carried the car swiftly across the tarmac toward the nearby Gulf Stream. Howling Mad Murdock was in the cockpit of the jet, gunning the engines and familiarizing himself with the instruments. The Face Man let down the swinging stairway and climbed down, reaching the asphalt just as Hannibal pulled up alongside him.

"Let's hurry and get him aboard," Hannibal said, gesturing to B.A., who was dozing inertly in the front seat. With the added help of the Face Man, Amy and Hannibal had a slightly easier time maneuvering B.A.'s bulk out of the car and up the steps leading to the plane. Down the runway Lynch's caravan was closing in, still flashing roof lights and sounding sirens.

"Do you have to do this every time B.A. flies?" Amy asked as they hefted the mechanic up the last few steps and into the plane.

"Kinda silly, isn't it?" Hannibal said with a grin.

"This is a notch or two past silly," Amy gasped. "This is ridiculous!"

Once they were all inside the plane, Peck pulled up the steps and Murdock rolled the Gulf Stream onto the runway.

"Welcome to Air Chance," the Face Man wisecracked. "Sorry, but we're out of kosher dinners."

Through the plane's windows, Amy could see the three sedans screech to a stop and emit armed officers from their side doors. "Who is that, anyway?"

Hannibal spotted Colonel Lynch amid the M.P.'s drawing aim on their aircraft. "Oh, nothing to be worried about, really. Just file it under 'old business.' Let's go, Murdock! Let's kiss ourselves some clouds, pronto!"

"You got it!" Murdock lined up his sights along the runway, then set both throttles at full. The Gulf Stream belched with thrustful fury and dragged itself forcefully away from Lynch's goon squad. Shots rang out, and a few dinged off the sides of the jet, but none struck solidly enough to impede the takeoff. Moments later the nose of the aircraft tilted upward, and the wheels lost touch with the ground.

"Next stop, Mexico," the Face Man called out cheerfully to his traveling companions.

The A-Team was on its way.

FOURTEEN

No longer saddled with the role of Buster Hawthorn, Howling Mad Murdock's spirits soared as high as the jet he was jockeying into the stratosphere. The cowboy hat was nowhere to be seen, having been replaced by the wide-brimmed black baseball cap that made him look like today's answer to Bowery Boy Huntz Hall. His weathered flight jacket hung loosely on his gangly frame, which bounced up and down in the seat in time to the pounding beat of a rock tape blaring over a portable cassette player.

" 'My friends, they all say I'm a reeealll loooon,' " he sang out loudly as his hands flicked over the bank of gauges mounted on the instrument panel before him. " 'A big goooon, and an ugly babooooon!' "

The door to the pilot's cabin swung open, and the Face Man entered, wincing at the audio assault.

"Murdock!"

But Murdock was too engrossed in his duet with Mick Jagger to hear Peck. Tapping in time to the drumbeat on the player, Murdock wailed, " 'But that's alllllll right, in fact I really don't care, but that's alllllll riiiiight—' "

"Murdock!" Face screamed again, lunging into the vacant pilot's seat next to Howling Mad. He waved his arms to make sure he had Murdock's attention.

"Huh . . . what?" Murdock shot one arm out and turned down the volume on the tape player. He leveled off the Gulf Stream's flight course, then glanced over at the Face Man, nonplussed. "So what's up, my man? Besides us, heh heh . . ."

"You keep that routine up, Murdock, and we're all going to end up like B.A. when it comes to flying." The Face Man turned the tape down even softer before continuing. "Hannibal wanted me to tell you we're headed for Acapulco."

"That's easy for him to say," Murdock complained. "I didn't have time to get me some flight plans to Mexico. I called Triple A back at the nutbin, but they don't deliver."

"So where does that leave us? What are our options?"

"I could follow the coast all the way, but we don't have the fuel for that," Murdock said, pointing to the appropriate dial. "Our best bet is for me to swing by the airport and try to pick up a flight we could follow down. . . ."

"I was hoping you were going to say that." The Face Man grinned as he reached into the pocket of his sport coat and withdrew a notepad. "I made a few calls back before I picked you up. Let's see here . . . I have a three-thirty Aeronaves de Mexico into Acapulco and a four-ten Western . . . both out of LAX . . ."

As he thought it over, Murdock flew out over the Pacific, seeking out some air space where he could circle as unobtrusively as possible. Once he made up his mind, he banked the plane slightly and told the Face Man, in pidgin Spanish, "I think we go weeeth Westaaaairn, gringo. Nice colors on their jets. Very easy to see, and their pilots won't mind so much eff we hitchhike. Si?''

"This part of the show's your baby, Murdock," the Face Man said, patting Murdock on the back as he got up out of the chair. "We'll leave you to your work. Just don't go off the deep end on us, okay?''

"What movie are they showing back in first class?" Murdock asked.

"No movies, no meals, Murdock.''

"Well, I don't want any complaints outta the passengers. That wasn't my idea.''

The Face Man rolled his eyes and departed from the pilot's cabin. No sooner had he closed the door than he heard the volume rise on the tape player as Murdock launched himself into another verse of "Jumping Jack Flash.''

In the passengers' cabin of the jet, Hannibal Smith was securing B.A. tightly into place in one of the chairs, binding the mechanic's arms and legs in such a way to make sure he wouldn't be getting up.

"What's with Murdock?" Hannibal asked when he saw Face leave the pilot's chamber.

"He thinks we can make it all the way down if we tail that Western flight I was telling you about," the Face Man replied as he came over to help Hannibal double-check the knots and straps confining B.A.

"Excuse me," Amy said, looking on with puzzlement. "What are you doing?"

"It's very simple," Hannibal informed her calmly, "we're tying him up so he won't kill us if he comes to."

"I see," Amy said warily, still trying to figure out the A-Team's way of doing things. "Uh, excuse me again, but . . . isn't he one of you? I mean, isn't he on the team?''

"Yep," the Face Man told her proudly. "Ol' B.A. here could tinker with an Edsel and make it win the Indy 500. We'd be lost without him.''

In his own defense, B.A. let loose a snore as loud as a buzz saw.

"I still don't understand," Amy said. "Why did you have to drug him?''

"He hates the pilot, and he's afraid to fly," Hannibal told her. "It's kind of a long story.''

"Hates the pilot?" Amy said. "Why?''

"Because our pilot is insane," the Face Man said.

"I know," Amy said worriedly. "I met him. Is he up there, flying us now?''

"Yep." Satisfied that B.A. was immobilized for the rest of the flight, Peck and Hannibal both eased back into their own seats. They hadn't had more than a few seconds of relaxation when the door to the pilot's cabin opened once more and Murdock strolled down the aisle toward them, hands in his pockets as he whistled to himself.

"Murdock!" the Face Man shouted, bolting from his seat and dragging the unbalanced aviator back to the controls.

Hannibal saw the look of abject terror on Amy's face and chuckled. "Too bad you didn't charge your tickets on your American Express card. You'd have automatic flight insurance.''

"How comforting of you to mention that," Amy said, nervousness apparent in her voice.

When the Face Man returned from his errand, he also tried to offer Amy some solace. "What a kidder," he joked. "Had it on automatic pilot . . . I think.''

"Where are the parachutes?" Amy asked, looking around the cabin.

"Well, this is just a demo model, remember," the Face Man said. "They might be back in storage. If you'd like, I could go check."

"I don't think I want to know," Amy said. Wringing her hands in her lap, she continued, "I'm not sure I like any of this. I'm not sure you're what I bargained for."

"You thought you were getting the Toluca Lake Boys' Choir?" Hannibal asked her as he peeled the cellophane off a fresh cigar.

"I . . . I don't know what I thought," Amy muttered.

Hannibal tested the aroma of the cigar, then slid it into his mouth and spoke around it. "Let's get something straight right now. You want your friend back. The authorities wouldn't give you the time of day, so you went out and hired a buncha gunfighters, namely us." He paused long enough to bite one tip off the cigar. "If you wanted somebody with nice manners, you should have hired an English butler."

Amy kept quiet a moment, struggling to get a proper perspective on her situation. None of her dealings with the A-Team had been remotely normal, and she was wondering how fine a line the whole group of them were treading between eccentricity and madness.

"Murdock . . . is he *really* insane?" she asked Hannibal.

"We think so." Hannibal spoke through a smoke ring. As the ring faded, he beamed proudly and boasted, "But he can fly this bird upside down under a suspension bridge if he has to. And the Face Man here . . . well, he's just the best song and dance man to ever hit town. Like Face just told you, ol' Sleeping Beauty over there can make machinery talk. We cover all the bases."

"Are you guys really being chased by the government?" Amy wanted to know.

"Is the fox always chased by the hound?" the Face Man responded. "Is the taxpayer really being chased by the IRS?"

"Did the dish really run away with the spoon?" Hannibal put in, growing more ash on the end of his cigar. Outside the plane, clouds were hugging the windows now. The engines throbbed with steady power.

"Why did you do it?" Amy said.

"Do what?" Hannibal asked.

"Why did you decide to help me?"

Inspecting Amy, Hannibal said, "Because you needed our help; because you wear expensive shoes that you didn't buy at a P.X." He reached over and tapped the crystal covering the timepiece on her wrist. "That's not a government-issue watch."

"I don't see what you're getting at."

Hannibal blew another puff of smoke. "Anyone with a French provincial living room probably isn't working for the government."

"Hold on a second!" Amy's temper suddenly flared into action. "You went through my house?"

"Listen, Miss Allen," the Face Man told her forcefully. "We have a problem. We don't do stuff like that because we're jerks. We have to make sure our clients aren't bird dogs for Colonel Lynch, that's all."

"We also agreed to help you when nobody else would," Hannibal joined in. "We're not asking for your thanks, but it'd be nice if you could get your eyebrows down from the middle of your forehead. We're not mutants from outer space, after all."

"I believe you," Amy said. "I believe you were sent into Hanoi under orders . . . that you are victims of a horrible mistake . . ."

"Very good," Hannibal applauded lightly. "You've done your homework."

"What I can't understand is why you all aren't just living in Switzerland where it's safe for you."

"We aren't living in Switzerland, Miss Allen, because we aren't Swiss." Hannibal pried out the ashtray in his armrest and tapped his cigar over it before drawing another mouthful of smoke. He let it out like steam. "We're Americans. We have a little problem now, but we'll work our way out of it somehow, some year. In the meantime, we stick together and do what we know best. If we help you, we need to know you'll protect us . . . not sell us out. It's hard enough the way it is, without more trouble."

"You have my word," Amy promised.

"That's nice, but we'd also like your money," Hannibal said, reaching over for her purse. Amy tried to stop him, but he took it away from her and passed it to the Face Man. "Mr. Lee said you had a hundred and fifty thousand to finance this operation, right?"

It didn't take Face Man long to realize that Amy was carrying far less cash than advertised. "She's light, Hannibal . . ."

"The bank was closed and I was rushed," Amy said desperately. "I had to borrow what I could and I—"

"Twenty-five thousand and change," the Face Man counted out the final tally.

"You came up a little short, honey," Hannibal said, anger shaving sharp edges to his words. "Twenty-five grand won't keep us in jet fuel."

"I'm sorry . . ."

Hannibal let out a breath of disappointment as he looked over at the Face Man. "I think we ought to turn around and call it off."

"Mr. Smith," Amy pleaded. "Look, I said I'm sorry . . . I couldn't come up with the money, but Mr. Lee said he'd call and give me some advance warning."

"No, that isn't what he said," Hannibal disagreed.

"How do you know?" Amy demanded hotly. "You weren't there. He was sprouting proverbs all over the place. I could hardly understand him."

The Face Man turned away from Amy, already focusing his attention on alternative plans. He suggested to Hannibal, "We could set up the movie company again and try to get what we need from the Film Commission."

Hannibal made a dour face. "That's always such a hassle."

"We have to do something," the Face Man said.

"I promise I'll pay you when we get back. My word is good," Amy insisted. Seeing the doubt in the men's eyes, she groped for further reassurance she could offer them. She finally thought of something and dished it out with a smile. "Women and people of high birth are very trust-worthy. I got that from Mr. Lee."

It was Hannibal's turn to smile. Adopting the Chinese accent of the fictitious laundromat owner, he corrected, "The Master say: 'Women and people of low birth are hard to deal with.' "

Amy looked hard at Hannibal as the realization slowly sank in. "I'll be damned . . ."

"No," Hannibal told her, "you'll be a princess in a world full of dragons."

FIFTEEN

Not wanting to draw suspicion from the Western Airline pilots, Murdock trailed the southbound jumbo jet from a discreet distance, occasionally letting the 747 ease out of sight before gunning the Gulf Stream's engines to catch up again. Hours slipped by, and the California coastline gave way to the sunbaked countryside of the Mexican mainland. They were flying at an altitude affording a clear view of the rolling hills, scattered villages, and verdant patches of plant life surviving on the harsh terrain. Lago de Chapala shone wetly in the hills south of Guadalajara, the largest body of water in the vicinity. The Sierra Madre Occidental mountain range gave way to the Sierra Madre del Sur, and off in the distance the faint glimmer of the ocean told the members of the A-Team that they would soon be arriving in Acapulco.

"Just a thought," the Face Man said, leaning away from the window. "Anybody here know any Spanish?"

Amy said, "I know my way around Mexican entrees on a restaurant menu, but that's about it."

"You're doing better than me, I'm afraid," Hannibal said. "All I know how to do is to cheer at a bullfight."

"Murdock's been spewing the lingo right and left since we took off, but I don't think he knows what he's saying," the Face Man said. "I think he's just parroting what he picks up on the radio. Well, Amy, it looks like you're our interpreter."

"I'm sure most of Acapulco's bilingual . . . at least I hope it is." Amy glanced over at B.A., who was beginning to stir in his seat. "What about him? Maybe he knows some."

"He's still working on English, Miss Allen." Hannibal sniggered.

"I'd keep my voice down if I were you, Hannibal," the Face Man warned. "Take a look; I think he's starting to wake up."

Hannibal went over to check up on B.A., who was rolling his head back and forth and sputtering dully to himself. Hannibal shook his head worriedly and moved away, telling the Face Man, "Must be he's building up a tolerance. That's not a good sign."

"He comes to, he's gonna bust those straps," the Face Man muttered bleakly. "Then he's gonna feed us our shoes."

Hannibal checked his watch, then excused himself from the others and made his way to the pilot's cabin, where, as the Face Man had already warned him, he found Murdock jabbering along to the Latin disco tune playing over the portable player's radio. Hannibal switched off the portable and tuned in the main radio until it was picking up transmissions from the control tower at the airport in Acapulco.

"Hey, conquistador," Murdock whined, "you done usurped my tunes!"

"The sleeping giant awakes," Hannibal informed Murdock matter-of-factly. "How fast can you get us down?"

Panic bleached Murdock's face as he groped for the levers to begin the plane's descent. Licking his lips, he sputtered, "You just landed, brother."

Over the cockpit intercom, the crackling voice of an air controller came to life, filled with urgency. "Unidentified aircraft behind Western one-six, heavy. Left hand climbing . . . turn immediately."

The words poured out of the speaker and toppled over one another, losing their meaning in the thick accent of the man who had spoken them. "Say what, muchacho?" Murdock shouted, flipping toggle switches and grabbing the radio microphone linking him up with the unseen control tower.

"Western heavy . . . abort . . . abort . . . Unidentified aircraft on starboard," came the garbled response.

"*No comprendo*, sweetheart," Murdock barked, yanking off his headset and allotting his full attention to the instruments around him.

"Aren't you supposed to talk to that guy?" Hannibal said, tensing in the seat adjacent to Murdock.

"We got the Cisco Kid in the tower, man! He might as well be talking native for all I can make out!" Murdock tugged down the brim of his flying cap, giving a look of intense concentration. "I'm just hopin' he gave me the green light to squeeze past that jumbo, 'cause that's the next item on this puddle jumper's agenda!"

Hannibal picked up the microphone connected to the speakers in the next cabin and announced, "This is the head steward. We'll be landing shortly, so please extinguish all smoking materials."

Murdock grabbed hold of one lever, then another, but ultimately pulled his hand away from both without throwing them. "Dang! Which one of these suckers is the reverse throttle lever, anyway?"

Noting his pilot's consternation, Hannibal brought the microphone to his mouth again and said, "Those of religious persuasion are encouraged to pray at this time . . ."

Up ahead, the 747 was responding to commands from the air control tower and veering its course slightly, giving Murdock room to whizz by and bring the Gulf Stream into landing position. The faded tar of the airstrip seemed to lunge up at them, taking bites at the small jet's tires. Murdock banked his luck on one of the levers and snapped it into service.

There was a loud blast as the engines fired into reverse, and the plane touched down for good, grinding to a rough halt in the middle of the runway. If anyone would have been cooking up eggs on the plane's kitchenette at the time, they would have come up scrambled by the time the jet stopped vibrating from the disruptiveness of its landing.

Once he was sure they'd stopped, Hannibal opened his eyes and slowly removed his fingernails from the cushion of his chair. Turning to Murdock, he said, "I think we're gonna have trouble with the airport on this landing."

"They can't do anything to me," Murdock crooned, pleased with his performance. "I'm escaped from a mental institution. It's not my fault. I don't even have a license anymore. I don't think I should be flying at all."

"Well, you're on the ground now, soldier," Hannibal told him. "Drive this thing to a parking space before that jumbo swoops down and swats us out of its way."

"You got it, boss . . ."

As Murdock got the Gulf Stream rolling off the runway and into the nearest taxi area, an official-looking white limousine broke away from a row of similar-looking cars parked next to the control tower. By the time the jet had been brought to a stop, the limousine was screeching to a halt beside it. The car door opened, and out climbed a thin, balding man in a short-sleeved uniform.

"Well, at least it isn't Lynch," Hannibal said, swiveling his chair around and heading out of the cabin. "Better bring your headset, Murdock. We're going to have to do some fast improv here, and we'll need all the props we can get."

"No props on this plane," Murdock said. "This sucker runs on turbines, and they got nothing to do—"

"Murdock, make yourself useful!"

In the other cabin B.A. had almost been jarred into consciousness. He was groaning miserably, like a man about to wake up from a bad dream. Hannibal moved over and helped the Face Man unstrap their mechanic, then help him to his feet.

"You got the script?" he asked Peck.

"The script? . . . Oh, that!" the Face Man said, recalling the earlier plan he'd mentioned. "Yep. Film Commission down here is run by a guy named Miguel Perez, if I remember rightly. I think our best bet is the sexy dumb blonde movie."

"The what?" Amy said, following behind Hannibal and the Face Man.

"You'll find out in time," Hannibal told her, taking one hand off B.A. long enough to snatch an oxygen mask dangling from its holding place above the seats. Pointing to a portable fire extinguisher on the other side of the cabin, he ordered, "Murdock, grab that and turn the label so people'll think it's pumping O_2."

"Aha!" Murdock said, catching on. "Brilliant stratagem, sir."

"Okay," Hannibal announced once Murdock had grabbed the extinguisher and moved ahead to the door. "Let's get this poor heart attack victim outta here on the double!"

Before leaving the plane, the A-Team polished up their paramedic routine. Peck played the doctor in charge, taking the headset from Murdock and burying the plug end into B.A.'s muscular flesh, giving the impression that he was making use of some updated version of the stethoscope. Hannibal continued to prop up Baracus from the other side while holding the black satchel containing various wares the A-Team would be relying on during their upcoming mission. As far as those on the ground were concerned, though, the valise was crammed with medical instruments.

"Do you want me to be a nurse?" Amy asked.

"Not unless it's necessary," Hannibal told her. "This kind of ad-libbing only comes from years of practice and being together so we know each other's timing. Our biggest problem now is making sure B.A.'s a good patient. Okay, Murdock, open the hatch and let's do it!"

The glare of sunlight outside the plane was oppressive, but not nearly as much as the glare in the eyes of the Mexican authorities comprising the welcoming reception. The balding man was surrounded by larger officers who had just arrived upon the scene and looked famished for a good confrontation. They all, save for the older man, carried guns and nightsticks.

"What is the meaning of—"

"Heart attack," Hannibal interrupted the Mexican. "We tried to call the town but couldn't get through."

Unappeased, the senior officer pointed an angry finger at the Gulf Stream and declared, "This plane is being impounded for illegal landing. Who is the pilot?"

Hannibal showed no sign of being impressed by the

other man's display of authority. Helping the Face Man drag B.A. across the blistering tarmac, he demanded of the Mexican, "What's your name, please?"

"Ground Control Officer Sanchez," the man snapped back. "Who's the pilot of this aircraft?"

With a tug of his head, Hannibal gestured to B.A., whose eyelids were beginning to flutter. Life was starting to surge through Baracus's lax muscles. Peck and Hannibal picked up their pace as best they could, easing their comrade toward the nearest airport limousine. Sanchez paced alongside them, venting more of his spleen.

"Your names and identification, please. I insist!"

"This man is dying!" Hannibal raged back at the officer. When Sanchez reeled back from the verbal onslaught and kept silent, Hannibal looked over at Peck, who was toying with the headset. "Tell me, how's his pulse, Doctor?"

The Face Man listened through the earphones, but the vital sign he was most concerned about was the strength awakening in B.A.'s limbs. Baracus was starting to walk instead of being dragged toward the limousine. "Not good," Peck told Hannibal. "We better hurry or it's gonna be all over."

Murdock rushed past the others and yanked open the back door of the limousine, then helped Hannibal and Peck negotiate B.A. inside. Sanchez came over, some of the fury knocked out of his sails.

"Nobody said anything about a heart attack," he said, almost apologetically. "We weren't told."

"Of course you weren't," Murdock yelled at him. "We didn't want to panic the passengers."

"What passengers?" Sanchez asked, looking back at the deserted plane.

"I was a passenger," Amy volunteered, sneaking Hannibal a triumphant wink.

"What?" Sanchez exclaimed.

"Officer Sanchez, this man's dying," Hannibal repeated with increased gravity. "Where's the nearest hospital?"

Officer Sanchez pointed past the unmoving group of men who had joined him near the jet. "That way, on the main road to town. It's only a few minutes away from here."

"Thank God for that," Hannibal said, squeezing into the back seat next to B.A. as Face circled around to get in the other side. Amy got into the front passenger's seat while Murdock went to the driver's side and held a hand out as he shouted, "Keys please."

Sanchez hesitated, closing his fist around the set of keys in his hand.

"Pulse is dropping!" the Face Man called out frantically. "We're gonna need life-support systems. This guy's almost dead!"

"Keys!" Murdock screamed again.

Sanchez reluctantly pried one key loose from the others in his hand and relinquished it to Murdock, who promptly took over the controls of the limousine and started up the engine. In the back seat, Hannibal rolled down his window and called out, "We'll see that you get a commendation for this, Officer Sanchez."

The limousine shot down the edge of the runway, leaving a wake of exhaust. Sanchez stared at the retreating vehicle a moment, then looked to his fellow officers and said, "A commendation from who? Who are those people?"

Murdock drove like a maniac, putting as much distance as possible between the limousine and the airport. The road they sped down was surrounded by lavish scenery;

deep blue lagoons, thick overgrowth, and, off in the distance, the aqua green of the ocean, which filled the air with its briny essence. The jostling of the uneven roadway shook B.A. until his eyes finally opened for the first time in hours.

"Where are we, man?" he moaned, squinting out the window over Hannibal's shoulder as he shook the final fog from his mind.

"Hey, B.A., welcome back!" Hannibal greeted him blithely. "You really slept, kid."

"Where are we?" B.A. asked again.

"Beautiful Acapulco," the Face Man told him. "Drove all night. You slept like a baby."

"That so?" B.A. mumbled suspiciously, blinking his eyes.

The Face Man yawned and stretched as much as he could in the cramped confines of the back seat. "It's a long ride, man. I wish one of these times you'd agree to fly. I'm stiff as a board."

B.A. grunted and lifted his arm up for a look at his wristwatch. The Face Man had already made sure to advance the date on its digital readout. "It's Friday already?"

"Right," Hannibal confirmed. "Musta been one of those little anxiety blackouts I was warning you about, B.A. How ya feeling?"

B.A. checked his watch again, then glowered. "I don't feel like I slept for no twenty-six hours, man." Noticing Murdock behind the wheel for the first time, he leaned forward and bellowed, "And when'd you get here? And what're you doin? You can't drive, sucker!"

"I can't?" Murdock shrieked. "I can't!?" He quickly veered off onto the shoulder and stopped the car, then catapulted out of the seat, leaving the keys in the ignition.

"All right, I'll drive," the Face Man said.

"No way, man," B.A. said, holding Peck back and climbing over the backrest into the driver's seat. "You musta all taken shifts but me gettin' down here. It's my turn and I'm gonna take it!"

"Whatever you say, B.A.," the Face Man said, staring down at the black fist wrinkling his shirtfront. The rings on Baracus's fingers looked like jewelled barnacles and were just as rough-edged as they poked through the cloth and dug into Peck's chest. "Just let me go before I get dimples on my rib cage, all right?"

B.A. withdrew his hand and took over the steering wheel as Murdock slid into the back seat. After taking a few deep breaths, Baracus felt well enough to drive, and he guided the limousine back onto the main road, passing the hospital. With the window down and the wind blowing full in his face, he was soon back to his old self. "So what's our battle plan, Hannibal?"

Hannibal fiddled with another cigar as he thought things over. Outside, Acapulco continued to unveil itself as a vacationer's paradise. It hardly seemed possible that treachery lurked in the surrounding hillsides and that the A-Team was here on a life-and-death mission rather than seeking out a good tan and cold margaritas.

"Okay, Face," Hannibal finally said, "you get us some digs and start throwing snowballs at the film commissioner. We're gonna probably need to scrounge up most of what we need since our client stiffed us."

"I said I was sorry," Amy said.

"That's all well and good, but it doesn't mean doodly squat at this stage," Hannibal reminded her. He paused to light up his cigar, then told the others, "B.A. is rested, so

I'll take him with me and Miss Allen. We'll get a line on Manny Cortez, then play it by ear . . .''

"Good enough," the Face Man said. "Murdock and I will handle the Film Commission."

"Yippee," Murdock said dryly as he went through Peck's valise and pulled out a dog-eared film script. "Oh, man, are we doing *Boots and Bikinis* again? I *hate* that movie! You ever read this script, Face? It stinks.''

"Yeah, well we're gonna keep makin' it till we get it right.''

B.A. let down on the gas and cruised down the fast lane leading to the shoreline, which was broken up by the sprouting forms of high-rise hotels and other buildings thriving off the touristas. "Friday already," he muttered again. "I musta slept like a brick.''

"You got a favorite hotel down here, Hannibal?" the Face Man asked.

"I'm a virgin here," Hannibal said. "Beats me."

"The Princess is nice," Amy suggested.

"You got it," the Face Man said.

SIXTEEN

The Princess was one of Acapulco's more prestigious hotels, a spacious building with indoor palms, crystal chandeliers the size of Volkswagens, and wide windows facing the sea. A landscaped horseshoe driveway connected the hotel with the main road, bordered by more palms maintaining a rigid vigil, armed with coconuts and long, feathery leaves, either of which could be dropped at the whim of the elements on unsuspecting pedestrians.

B.A. drove the airport limo up to the main entrance and shifted into neutral while the Face Man and Murdock climbed out. They'd both rummaged through one of the tourist shops down the street and bought outfits that smacked of Hollywood chic. As B.A. wheeled off with Hannibal and Amy, the two men swaggered up the walk and into the lobby as if they owned the place. A fastidious doorman intercepted them, his face fixed with a professional smile.

"Checking in, sir?" he asked the Face Man, his English accented but polished.

"I'm with Twentieth Century-Fox," Peck sniffed. "We're with the movie company."

"Begging your pardon?"

"The Farrah Fawcett, Bo Derek, Loni Anderson movie," the Face Man said impatiently. "Of course you've been told about it."

The doorman's smile went limp as he confessed, "I know nothing of this, señor. Perhaps at the desk?"

Murdock shook his head miserably, and the Face Man exhaled with the force of someone who'd just reached his limit of tolerance for incompetence. "Boy, there better not've been a foul-up on this," he fumed. "I'm telling you, my head'll roll if this deal got messed up, too. And I'll warn you right now, amigo, if I go down for this one, I'm taking some people with me!"

"But, señor, I am only a doorman!" the uniformed attendant pleaded. "Come, come. Let us speak to the desk people. They may be able to help!"

"Boy, I sure hope so," Murdock said. Taking the doorman aside, he whispered, "My partner's got one nasty temper. I'll try to keep a leash on him, but you better track down your bosses and warn them that when he goes berserk, he goes berserk. . . ."

"Sí," the doorman gasped frailly, scurrying off to consult with the receptionist before Peck or Murdock could reach the desk. Both men took their time getting there, giving the doorman a chance to convey the full situation.

"Man looks like he's got the fear of the Lord in him," the Face Man told Murdock. "What'd you say to him?"

"I told him you were a descendant of Cortez and that you like to stomp on people . . . or words to that effect."

"I hope you didn't lay it on too thick," Peck whispered, seeing the doorman rush off and disappear inside the nearby security office. "We're looking for a nice room, not a padded cell."

"We'll find out soon enough, hombre," Murdock said as they reached the desk.

"Greetings, gentlemen," the receptionist told them, all smiles. She was a young woman with finely sculpted features and hair the color of a raven's wings. Head to toe she reeked of poise and charm, and she was calling on all her resources to placate the men before her. "We haven't received any word regarding your company as of yet, but our assistant manager is just down the street at a conference meeting with the owners. I suspect they have probably already arranged for your lodging but merely forgot to inform us. It's not an uncommon occurrence. While you're waiting, perhaps you'd like to step into our lounge for drinks and some lunch."

Murdock and the Face Man traded glances but said nothing.

"There would be no charge, of course," the receptionist chimed in. "It's our way of apologizing for a momentary inconvenience until our assistant manager returns."

"Well, come to think of it, I *am* a little hungry," Peck said, rubbing his stomach and acting somewhat appeased. "How about you, Stoney?"

Murdock frowned a moment, then said, "I worked up a bit of a thirst coming here, I have to admit."

Just then the doorman emerged from the security office and ambled back to the receptionist's side. She told him, "Miguel, please take these gentlemen to the executive lounge and let them have their choice of booths. I'll call ahead to see that they're properly taken care of from there."

"Sí," the doorman said, stepping around the desk and motioning to a nearby archway. "Follow me, gentlemen, if you please . . ."

"Gladly," the Face Man said.

Murdock walked close beside Peck and hissed in his ear, "Stoney? Hell, that's worse than Buster. How's about calling me Joe or something normal for once, huh?"

"Maybe I could rename you after your Uncle Deke," Peck suggested.

"Forget it," Murdock grumbled. "Just say 'Hey you.' "

The executive lounge was a richly appointed room that extended out over a man-made lagoon filled with brightly colored fish and surrounded by equally stunning plants. The Face Man and Murdock chose a booth near the windows, then ordered up tequila sunrises while they browsed over the menus.

"So far so good," the Face Man said once the headwaiter left their table.

"Let's just hope they don't get any wise ideas about wiring back to the States," Murdock said, noticing three uniformed security officers enter the lounge and take up perches on bar stools on the other side of the room. They tried to appear nonchalant, but it was clear they were keeping an eye on the newcomers. "I'd hate to be in my shoes if someone blows our cover."

"Hey, don't sweat it," the Face Man said, leaning back in the booth. "Relax and enjoy the view. The hard part comes later."

"You think we should start asking around about Massey?" Murdock wondered. "I mean, it wouldn't surprise me if he spent some time here."

The Face Man shook his head. "That's Hannibal's department. We don't want to step on his lines."

The waiter returned with their drinks, then wandered off to tend to the next table. Peck raised his glass and proposed a toast. "To a new adventure."

"I'll drink to that." Murdock chinked Peck's glass with

his own, then sniffed the drink. "Smells safe." He drained the whole glass in one long swallow, then eyed the Face Man soberly and said, "If I fall over, run for it."

The Face Man watched on without touching his drink. Murdock's eyes began to swim slightly, but he remained upright in the booth. "How you feeling, Murdock?"

"Pickled tink," Murdock said. "Bring on the lobster . . ."

SEVENTEEN

While the Face Man and Murdock were dining in luxury, the rest of the A-Team was taking a tour of Acapulco's armpit, a run-down part of the city where the primary decor was boarded windows and shadows that teemed with ominous activities. Located far from the benefits of a refreshing ocean breeze, these mean streets were stirred up by a hot wind that smelled like the bad breath of El Diablo himself.

"Hey, man, I don't like this," B.A. said as he drove the airport limousine around the potholes dotting the road. In darkened doorways he could make out hungry children eyeing the vehicle's gleaming hubcaps. "This Massey dude musta had a nose for trouble to be hangin' around a place like this."

"He's a good reporter," Amy defended her missing associate. "If a story led him here, the looks of the area wouldn't stop him from checking things out."

"I still say if a man looks for trouble, he's gonna find it." B.A. slowed down on a signal from Hannibal and started inspecting storefronts for the one they were seeking.

"There it is," Hannibal said, pointing to a bleak-looking bar halfway down the block.

"What? There what is?" Amy asked as B.A. eased the limo over to the curb.

"We checked the phone number from Massey's notes while you were powdering your nose a few blocks back," Hannibal told her. "It belongs to this dive."

The three of them waited in the car a moment, watching the tavern. It had swinging, saloon-type doors, and an up-tempo Spanish love song poured out onto the dusty sidewalk from an unseen jukebox inside. No one had gone into or come out of the establishment since B.A. had pulled up.

"What do we do now, Hannibal?" B.A. asked, turning off the engine.

"You're the backup, so keep your eyes and ears open," Hannibal told him as he got out of the car and held the door open for Amy. "I'll go in and tip the joint over, see what happens."

B.A. nodded and rolled down his window, blinking away a gust of dust that immediately blew into his face.

" 'Tip the joint over,' " Amy chided mockingly as she stepped up to the sidewalk next to Hannibal. "That sounds very macho, but is it smart?"

"If I was smart, I wouldn't be working for some skirt with no money," Hannibal drawled, closing the car door.

B.A. grinned and leaned across the front seat, calling out to Amy, "You learn to love him, Mamma, but it takes a long time."

"That's what he said about you," Amy told B.A.

"Okay, okay, enough of this mutual admiration crap," Hannibal said. "We've got work to do."

Amy turned her head away from the wind and took a

deep breath to settle her nerves, then followed Hannibal into the bar. It was tidier inside, but not by much. Few of the tables or chairs matched, and the bare walls were scarred and dented from years of brawling. A handful of locals were scattered about the room, and they all stopped talking once the Americans came in. The song on the jukebox scratched its way to the end, and no music took its place. The only sound in the tavern was the creaking whir of a portable fan and the hollow sound of Amy's heels connecting with the faded planks that lined the floor. Amy was terrified, but Hannibal took it all in with a loopy grin that smacked of confidence without regard for tact.

"This dump looks long on local color and short on blended whiskey," he said, loud enough for all to hear.

Amy winced at the remark and moved close to Hannibal, whispering, "I hope you have some sort of plan."

Hannibal offered her a wink of self-assurance on his way to the bar. The man tending the bar was middle-aged, with a faint bulge in his gut from too much beer, but there were taut, corded muscles lining his exposed arms. A swizzle stick was clenched between his teeth, its pointed end sticking out like a devil's tongue. "Hey, señor," he advised, "this bar is not for American tourists."

"Glad to hear it," Hannibal replied calmly, loosening his collar. "Kinda hot out there. You got a couple beers?"

"We got nothing for you, 'cept a warning," the bartender told him as he took the swizzle stick from his mouth and snapped it between his thick fingers. "You go now. Plenty cantinas down at the beach."

A subdued murmuring broke out among the other locals as they set down their beers and flexed their hands before closing them into fists. Hannibal leaned on the bar and turned to face the others, motioning Amy to his side as he called out, "I'm looking for a man named Manny Cortez."

The whisperings dwindled to a renewed silence.

"So you know him, eh?" Hannibal guessed. "Well, good. Good deal. I got money. I'm willing to pay anybody who can help me find him."

Hannibal didn't get the reaction he'd been hoping for. The man closest to the door grabbed a thick slab of wood and placed it in front of the opening, then slipped an even thicker bar into place across it, closing off the bar. The others shifted across the floor, fanning out to surround Amy and Hannibal.

"Is this in the plan?" she asked him worriedly.

Hannibal ignored the question, concentrating on the mini-mob closing in on them. To Amy's surprise he suddenly began to speak to the other men in their native tongue. *"Escuchame . . . no quiero hacer daño a nadie solomente trato hallar ese hombre."*

Again Hannibal's strategy backfired. Stepping around from behind the bar, the bartender said, "We are not children who are impressed that you speak our language . . . and now it is time to teach you the lesson you have come for."

Her voice trembling, Amy asked, "Hannibal, is this—"

"No," he snapped, cutting her off. Moving away from the bar to the center of the room, he met the hateful gazes of the men surrounding him. "Okay, you want tough? You got tough. I came here in friendship. I want only to speak to Manny Cortez."

The bartender grinned, but it wasn't an expression of amusement. "We will find out what you want . . ."

Through the grime-layered window next to the main

doorway, Hannibal spotted the outline of a familiar figure and promptly shouted, "B.A., get in here! I got trouble!"

Hannibal's cry served to momentarily distract the others, giving B.A. time to summon his full strength and bring it to bear against the unwieldy board blocking the door. Both the board and the wooden bar holding it in place splintered loudly and fell away, leaving B.A. standing in the doorway, a figure of imposing menace. He glared at the locals as he strode forcefully to the middle of the room, joining Hannibal and Amy.

The locals retreated a few steps but showed no signs of leaving the bar. The bartender cupped one hand next to his mouth and yelled in the direction of the kitchen, "*Quintana! Ven acá! Ándale!*"

There was a sound of rattling dishes in the back room, then the door leading to the kitchen opened and Mexico's answer to Bigfoot lumbered into the bar. He was nearly seven feet tall and had arms the size of most men's legs. His sleeves were rolled up from washing dishes, and his dishpan hands were as large as clumps of bronzed bananas. His brawn came at the expense of his brains, but it didn't take him long to figure out why he'd been called. He looked the three gringos over like a glutton eyeballing a three-course dinner.

Amy cleared her throat to ask Hannibal something, but he waved her silent and said, "No!"

"I didn't think so," Amy murmured.

Quintana the Giant stepped up to B.A., and the two men sized each other up. The Mexican struck the first blow, lashing out with a punch that snapped B.A.'s head back but left him standing still. Acting as if nothing had happened, B.A. looked over at Hannibal and asked, "You want him?"

Hannibal thought it over, then said, "Nah, you take him."

B.A. sent a ringed fist crashing into Quintana's midriff, but it seemed to have even less effect than the blow B.A. had received. With the first blows traded, the real fighting began in earnest. Hannibal quickly shoved Amy aside, then threw himself at the locals, waging a one-man offensive that was part martial arts, part big-time wrestling, and part free-for-all. He sent men flying against the furniture, some of them dropping to the floor, but there were too many of them to handle alone. Amy tried to even up the odds with a few well-placed swings of a hastily grabbed beer bottle, but the bartender finally managed to come up behind her and pull her aside. Hannibal was tackled, disappearing from view in the clot of Mexicans holding him down, while B.A. waged a valiant but futile prizefight with Quintana. The larger man's longer reach finally won the day, wearing down B.A.'s endurance to the point where a particularly vicious uppercut caught B.A. off guard and turned his world into a swirl of taffy that faded quickly to black. . . .

EIGHTEEN

The dust in the cantina had long settled by the time Hannibal and B.A. surfaced from their respective dreamlands and found themselves bound to two of the three chairs that had somehow avoided demolition during the earlier melee. Amy was tied to the third one. She hadn't been roughed up too severely, but, like Hannibal and B.A., she was gagged and being watched closely by the bartender and Quintana and a few of the other men who had lent a hand tying knots.

There was a stranger in the ravaged bar, too, and he paced before the prisoners, visibly agitated. When he saw Hannibal and B.A. coming back to their senses, he signaled for Quintana to untie the gags. While the giant went about his task, clumsily fingering knots, the stranger perused the contents of Amy's wallet and pulled out her press card.

"Amy Allen," he read with only a faint native accent. "Los Angeles *Courier-Express* . . ."

"If I might explain," Hannibal began, speaking awkwardly to compensate for his bruised jaw.

On the stranger's signal, Quintana demonstrated how his

hands could make a necklace around Hannibal's throat. It was a tight fit, and Hannibal got the message, closing his mouth.

"I wasn't talking to you, chico, so keep it still," the stranger warned Hannibal. After Hannibal nodded, Quintana eased his grip and stepped back. The stranger turned his attention back to Amy. "Why do you want Manny Cortez?"

With the back of her hand Amy rubbed the taste of wet rags from her mouth, then told the stranger, "I'm looking for a friend of mine. His name is Al Massey. He also worked for the *Courier* and he was down here on a story when he suddenly—"

"What kind of story?" the stranger asked.

"I don't know," Amy admitted. "That's what we were—"

"I thought you were close friends. . . ."

"We are!" Amy insisted. She tried to get out of her chair and almost toppled over. Quintana reached out and steadied the chair, giving Amy a threatening growl. She made an indignant face at the giant, then looked back at the stranger. "That was his way . . . always secretive. I just know he came down here and disappeared. I want to find him."

The stranger glanced at the other locals and said, *"Es la verdad, mi amigo mi dijo de esta chica."*

Hannibal had had his fill of token submissiveness. Clearing his throat, he called out defiantly, "Okay, so Al Massey told you about her. That cleans her up, but it doesn't tell us who you are, sonny."

Amy shot Hannibal a confused glance. "I thought you said you didn't know Spanish."

"Professional modesty," Hannibal said. Eyeing their

interrogator, he repeated, "So will the mystery guest please sign in?"

"I'm the man you so desperately seek, señor," the stranger informed them. "I am Manny Cortez."

Hannibal beamed at B.A. and Amy. "I just love it when a plan comes together!"

"Hey, I got loose teeth on account of this plan of yours, sucker," B.A. complained.

"You'll have to forgive my friends," Manny explained to the prisoners as he took a knife off the nearby counter and used it to cut free the Americans. "They say you were not very clear about why you wanted me. They were trying to protect me."

Once his hands were free, Hannibal wiped his fingers across his chafed wrists to soothe the burning. He said to the man with the knife, "And exactly who are you? . . . besides Manny Cortez, that is."

As he cut Amy's bonds, Manny said, "Al Massey was my friend also. He told me of the little chica who works with him at the paper. He mentioned your name several times."

Both Hannibal and B.A. groaned as they stood up and felt for broken bones. "Man, I feel like I've been through the wringer, Hannibal," B.A. said, keeping a wary eye on Quintana, who smiled pridefully, as if he understood English and was pleased with the compliment.

"Again I apologize for this reception," Manny said, setting the knife back on the counter. "But I am a marked man. Valdez has agents in Acapulco . . . everywhere. I must be very careful."

"What about Al?" Amy asked. "Is he okay?"

Manny hesitated, falling back to his pacing. "I cannot say. I do not think so. I have said prayers in church."

"Is he dead?" B.A. asked.

Manny sighed and ran his hand through his dark hair. Avoiding Amy's searching gaze, he reflected, "He saved me from this butchering drug peddler Malavida Valdez. Al Massey perhaps gave his life so I could live . . . this was truly a great man."

"Oh, my God . . ." Amy said, her legs quivering. Hannibal hurried over and helped her back into her chair.

"Easy, Amy," he comforted her. "He said 'perhaps.' "

"This is true," Manny said. "There is a chance he still lives. There is a chance. We will talk about it tonight."

"I hope he's okay," Amy wished aloud. "He just has to be!"

"For now, we must wait," Manny said. "Do you people have lodging?"

"Well, that's kinda hard to say just yet," Hannibal told him. "We have some people working on that. . . ."

NINETEEN

Peck and Murdock had worked it out nicely.

When B.A. drove back to the Princess Hotel an hour later and pulled up to the main entrance, the Face Man pushed out the doors, grinning like a man who'd just been given the key to the city. Murdock followed close behind, hands in his pockets and exuding an air of decadent leisure.

As the doorman closed in on the limousine, the Face Man headed him off, telling him, "These are my people, chickie. They like to take care of themselves."

"As you wish, señor," the doorman said, taking a step back and watching the other members of the A-Team pile out of the limousine. His eyes widened when they fell on the bejewelled, Mohawk presence of B. A. Baracus.

"What you lookin' at, sucker?" B.A. demanded, circling around the car and looming in front of the doorman.

"Ohhhhhh, nothing. Nothing, señor."

"Good, 'cause I don't like people gawking at me." B.A. handed the doorman the keys to the limousine, adding, "Here . . . you got nothing better to do, have somebody clean up my car. I don't want nobody writing 'Wash Me' in Spanish on my fenders, dig?"

The doorman bobbed his head demurely and slinked off to confer with the nearest valet while B.A. reached into the back seat for the luggage they'd bought and filled with clothes on the way to the hotel. A few feet away, the Face Man was putting on a show to maintain the team's cover as a film crew. Embracing Hannibal in a big Hollywood hug, he oozed with tinsel enthusiasm.

"Andre, sweetheart. *Cómo esta,* boobala?"

"Nice to see you again, too, wunderkind," Hannibal said, patting Peck on the back. "You made arrangements all right, I gather?"

The Face Man broke their embrace and offered Amy a swift wink before pulling Hannibal aside for some hushed conversation. "Fires burning all over, Hannibal. This joint's packed. Assistant manager's some schmoe named Rodriguez. Always has his hand out and likes to beat on his help. He'll be a tough nut to crack. Then there's a guy from the Film Commission with a case of terminal hots."

"Hmmm," Hannibal said. "Still have some fast talking to do, then, eh?"

"Sí," the Face Man said. "You're Andre Brusae . . . big megabuck director, just coming off a hot slasher flick. You're executive producer, too, so we all hang on your every word . . ."

"Love it," Hannibal said, firing up another cigar.

Murdock and B.A. headed up the congregation as they entered the lobby. Amy and the Face Man flanked Hannibal, who took in the large, open space and started framing potential shots with his thumbs. "Hmmmmmm," he contemplated, thinking aloud, "we'll wanna green this entrance. God, where do they get those scruffy little palm trees?"

This was said within earshot of Assistant Manager Jose

Rodriguez, a meticulously dressed man with a bricklayer's build and a lumpy face that quaked with each display of emotion. He was in the midst of a verbal assault on a cowering bellboy half his age. He wrapped that up, then adjusted his lapels and drifted over to where Hannibal was throwing a temper tantrum of his own.

"Man, one foul-up after another. I got no help at all out there this afternoon. Shirley's sick. Wardrobe is still trying to trace two lost crates full of Bo's ball gowns . . ." Hannibal's cigar was burning fast in his mouth, like a short fuse. As the Face Man picked up a nearby ashtray and held it out to catch the grey fallout, he cringed convincingly in the face of Hannibal's posed ire. "I gotta tell ya, bunkey, you're hangin' by a thread with me. I never seen such crappy preproduction in fifteen years of making boffo blockbusters."

"I'm sorry, Mr. Bursae," Peck whimpered. "I'm really sorry."

As the assistant manager entered their midst, Murdock drifted away, disappearing into a small arcade next to the receptionist's desk. Amy and B.A. stayed with the group, but eased back to give Hannibal and the Face Man room to work their jive.

"Greetings," Rodriguez said with guarded politeness. He asked Peck, "These are the people you spoke of?"

"Precisely," the Face Man said. "Andre Bursae, I'd like you to meet Jose Rodriguez. He's the assistant manager of the Princess."

Hannibal darted his right hand out. "How ya doin', Jo?"

"Jose, Mr. Bursae," Rodriguez corrected. "I'm afraid there's been some kind of mistake. Apparently we were

not notified that your motion picture company was expected.''
He refrained from shaking Hannibal's hand.

Hannibal slowly ground out his cigar in such a way to indicate he'd like to do the same with Peck. He dropped his smile and turned on Rodriguez. ''I hope you're not telling me we got no rooms, Joey, because if that's what you're telling me, I'm gonna raise some hell. The Mexican government pleads with me to come down here and help prop up the peso, but since I got here, it's been one screw-up after another.''

As Rodriguez shifted slightly on his feet and deliberated a response, another man joined the group. He was fat but poised, his black hair neatly slicked back around his ears. He wore thick-rimmed tinted glasses and a cream-colored leisure suit that might have been in style for a few weeks ten years ago.

''Andre, this is Miguel Perez,'' the Face Man told Hannibal. ''He's head of the Film Commission here.''

Perez held out a hand, but it was Hannibal's turn to remain aloof. ''You're really sinking my boat, Mike,'' he told the commissioner, who slowly pulled his arm back to his side. ''I was told this was all gonna be greased. Since I got down here this morning, ain't one thing been right.''

Perez looked over at Rodriguez and licked his lips nervously. While Hannibal and the Face Man waited for an answer, B.A. took Amy by the crook of the arm and led her away, leaving the luggage behind.

''I don't believe this,'' Amy said.

''Face Man's got 'em goin','' B.A. said with obvious admiration. ''He hits 'em with a right and Hannibal comes back with a left cross. We're gonna get some good digs, count on it. C'mon, let's grab some grub.''

On their way to the lounge, B.A. and Amy looked in at

the arcade, where Murdock had gathered a flock of preteen fans around the video game he was beating into submission. "C'mon, c'mon, here we go!" Murdock cheered himself on, commandeering his joystick as if World War III were on the line. "Vipers at two o'clock!"

"I have to hand it to you guys," Amy told B.A. as they left Murdock to his throng. "You have your own way of doing things."

"And we get results, too," B.A. boasted. "Don't forget that!"

Back in the lobby, Perez huddled briefly with Jose, then the assistant manager excused himself to tend to some business behind the main desk.

"Uh, Mr. Bursae," Perez said, showing Hannibal a mouthful of nicotine-stained teeth. "Andre, if I may . . . sometimes communication between our office and the States gets a little . . . how you say . . . garbled?"

Hannibal held up his hand like a traffic cop. "Hey, chickie, next thing I'm gonna hear is you didn't even know this ten-million-dollar film was coming down here."

"Well, now that you mention it . . ."

Hannibal let out a warning sigh and turned his back to Perez, concentrating on framing a few more shots of the lobby. Peck looked desperately at the film commissioner and pantomimed slitting his own throat. Perez shrugged his shoulders futilely.

"Andre," the Face Man said, putting a hand on Hannibal's shoulder. "They're trying to clear some rooms for Bo, Farrah, and Loni. Fifteenth floor, ocean side. They're gonna work on getting one for you, too, and . . . hell, you know me, I can bunk anywhere."

The news seemed to have a calming effect on Hannibal, but Rodriguez rejoined the group moments later to burst the balloon. "I'm afraid I won't be able to help you," he apologized. "It's such short notice. Mrs. Onderdonk won't move. We have the Insurance Conventioneers coming in tonight . . ."

Hannibal stared intently at Rodriguez, but the look in his eyes was not that of anger. He seemed preoccupied with another thought. "Hmmmmmm," he mumbled to himself.

"I'm sorry," Rodriguez said. "Perhaps another time . . ."

Hannibal patted his pockets, tracking down another cigar and pulling it out. As he readied it for smoking, he asked Rodriguez, "You ever do any acting, Jo?"

Rodriguez blinked with disbelief, and his demeanor abruptly changed from forced regret to giddy nervousness. "Uh . . . no, sir. No. Never," he stammered.

Hannibal moved fast while Rodriguez was ripe for the picking. "Would you do a nude love scene, Joey?"

Rodriguez squirmed in his shoes, his face turning the same shade of burgundy as his blazer. Visions of Loni Anderson danced in his head. "Uh . . . well, if the part required . . ."

Hannibal poked the cigar into his mouth and clamped down on it with a smile as he consulted with the Face Man. "Tell me, chickie, is Jo here right for El Tigre, or is he right for El Tigre?"

Peck looked at Rodriguez in a new light, and the worry faded from his face as he exclaimed, "God, Andre . . . is he ever! I can't believe I didn't see it before!"

"El Tigre?" Perez said, trying to make sense of the situation. "Who is this El Tigre?"

"Oh, he's only the second romantic male lead," the Face Man told him.

"How tall're you, Joey?" Hannibal asked Rodriguez.

Rodriguez fumbled through his blazer for a pack of matches and lit one, holding the flame so Hannibal could puff life into his cigar. "Five-eight, Mr. Bursae."

"Five-eight." Hannibal clucked his tongue around the cigar. "Bo is a shade taller. That's too bad."

"Actually, I'm five-eight-and-a-half," Rodriguez said quickly. "Almost five-nine."

Hannibal let out a plume of smoke and looked over the lobby one more time, then wrinkled his face with a look of resignation. "It doesn't really matter. We're sunk anyway. Let's round up the troops and get outta here."

"Excuse me, sir," Rodriguez said, taking a long step to block Hannibal's retreat. Gesturing toward the executive lounge, he offered, "If you would like to rest a moment, maybe have a drink on the house, I could try again to free up some rooms."

Hannibal thought it over, checking his watch. "I'll tell you what, Joey," he finally decided. "You get us in and you got the part of El Tigre."

Rodriguez's eyes lit up like twin fruits on a slot machine. Hannibal had just hit the jackpot.

TWENTY

Determined to earn his chance to get close to some prime
Hollywood flesh, Rodriguez camped out on the desk phone
trying to scrounge up rooms for the A-Team. He said it
would take some time and apologized for the delay. While
they were waiting for results, the Americans huddled together in one corner of the lobby to discuss their next
move. Hannibal and Peck decided to wait on Rodriguez
while the others left the hotel to look into renting a typewriter and buying a few other supplies they'd need to carry
on their charade as a film company. When B.A., Murdock,
and Amy returned to the lobby an hour later, Hannibal and
Peck were gone. So was Rodriguez. The receptionist gave
B.A. a note Hannibal had left on a map of the city,
pointing out an address they were to drive to immediately.

"Hey, man, what is this, a trick?" B.A. demanded,
leaning threateningly across the desk.

"I don't know, sir, I just came on a few minutes ago,"
the receptionist squeaked, leaning back in her chair and
holding onto the armrests for dear life. "I was just told to
give this to you when you came in. That's all I know."

"I don't like it, man," B.A. grumbled.

Murdock grabbed the map and looked over the writing. "It's Hannibal's writing, all right."

"Maybe the address is for another hotel," Amy suggested.

"Then why didn't he just say so?" B.A. said. "Man, it ain't like Hannibal to play games like this."

"Whoah, Nellie!" Murdock said, spotting more writing on the bottom corner of the map. "It says here, 'Gotta big surprise. Hurry and think first class.' "

"Lemme see that." B.A. inspected the note again, then grinned over at Amy. "What'd I tell ya? They got us some good digs."

"I sure hope so," Amy said, beginning to wonder.

A five-mile drive later, B.A.'s prediction was borne out. He pulled the washed limousine up a brick-laid driveway to a rambling, landscaped estate the size of a country club. Sculpted figurines spat streams of water in a large reflecting pool set before a tile and stucco mansion overlooking an unblemished stretch of coastline.

"This is incredible!" Amy gasped, taking it all in. "How do you guys do it?"

"Moxie," B.A. said, getting out of the limousine and heading up the flagstone walk. Amy and Murdock followed on either side of him. "Sometimes Hannibal does his jazz hot and sassy, other times he'll be smooth as silk—whatever it takes to get what needs gettin'."

"Where do I sign up for lessons?" Amy said with admiration as they paused before a pair of matching carved oak doors. A sparkling chain of bronze links dangled off to one side, and when Amy tugged it, a sweet sound of rich, resonant chimes reverberated throughout the house.

"It's open!" a familiar voice called out from within.

The threesome stepped into a luxuriously adorned hallway that branched off in a dozen directions, each one leading to rooms that looked like treasure troves filled with the amassed wealth of a pirate franchise. There were antiques, pieces of art, and furniture from all corners of the globe tastefully arranged in a manner geared to produce a quiet awe bordering on reverence. At the end of the hallway was a sliding glass door that opened out onto a railed veranda, where Hannibal and the Face Man sat in wicker chairs sipping frosted margaritas as they contemplated the coming sunset.

"Welcome to paradise," the Face Man told his friends as they stepped out onto the balcony.

"What happened?" Murdock asked. "This place looks like a year's worth of *Archy Digest* rolled into one pad."

"Yeah, Hannibal," B.A. said. "What gives, man?"

"How much is this costing us?" Amy wanted to know.

"Nothing. It's on the house," Hannibal said, pointing to a nearby tray filled with glasses and a half-filled pitcher of margaritas. "Sit down and drink up. It's been a good day so far."

"How'd you do it?" Amy asked as she started filling glasses.

Face explained, "Jose couldn't turn any rooms, so we had to settle on the owner's private villa. His name is Jorge. In the movie he plays the part of El Toro, El Tigre's rival for the heart of Farrah Fawcett."

"I see . . ." Amy sat down slowly and put her feet up before taking a sip of the margarita.

"Everyone's got their own room," the Face Man went on. "You'll find some more clothes in the bedroom closets. I tried to tell Jorge to let you pick out some things of your own, but he's big on surprises."

"That explains the note," B.A. said, wiping the salt moustache left on his lip after draining his first drink.

"Where is this Jorge now?" Murdock asked. "And Jose?"

Hannibal and Face looked at one another, sharing a laugh before Hannibal divulged, "They're on their way to Mexico City, by jet. Seems Jorge knows some trader up there that deals in potent aphrodisiacs. They want very much to be true Latin lovers."

"They're gonna be mad when all them stars you promised don't show up," B.A. said.

"Hopefully we'll be long gone by then," Hannibal replied.

"I at least hope we're going to do a different movie than *Boots and Bikinis*," Murdock said. "I *hate* that movie."

"So you've told us, Murdock. That's still our baby, though," Hannibal said, holding his glass out for Amy to refill. "Miguel Perez is reading the script on behalf of the Film Commission tonight. We're gonna need to fire him up and get him out there, beating the bushes. B.A., did you get ahold of a typewriter?"

"It's in the trunk," B.A. said. "Heavy sucker. Secretary size."

"Good, good," the Face Man said. "I'll get on the rewrites so we can hit Perez with them tomorrow."

"Rewrites?" Amy said. "I don't understand how this whole film scam works."

"You'll find out soon enough," the Face Man told her. "Basically, though, we do rewrites to come up with scenes that call for whatever equipment it is we think we'll be needing. The Film Commission foots the bill, and we keep our overhead down."

"Amazing," Amy said, shaking her head. "Do you guys do this all the time?"

Hannibal sampled his drink, thinking back. "No, we haven't done the film company in six months. Lot of logistics you have to keep your eye on all the time."

Amy got up from her chair and walked out to the railing. The sun had just touched the horizon, spreading its gold reflection across the placid sea. The slight breeze was already beginning to cool down for the night. Amy rubbed her arms to warm them, then turned around to face the four men she had hired. A tinge of guilt was beginning to prick at her conscience.

"What about the fact you're scamming a legitimate business?" she asked Hannibal. "Don't you feel bad about the people who get used by you?"

Halfway through his third margarita, Hannibal didn't look like he was feeling anything. "They're just making a contribution to the cause," he rationalized. "They'll help us find out what happened to your friend and maybe shut down this guy Valdez. Don't you think a couple of free rooms is a worthwhile donation? Nobody's getting hurt."

"I guess you're right," Amy said uncertainly.

"I know I'm right, Miss Allen," Hannibal assured her. "These people may not realize it, but we're giving them the chance to be heroes."

"Yeah," B.A. said with finality. "So be cool, woman."

The group sat silent for the next few minutes, finishing their drinks as the sun fell below the waterline and let the moon take over for the night. There was an outside fireplace on the veranda, already heaped high with kindling and pine logs. Murdock ignited the twigs, and soon a bright blaze was chasing away the nocturnal chill.

"What's our next move?" Amy asked, breaking the silence.

"We'll know that once we've had a chance to chat with Manny Cortez," Hannibal said. "He should be here any minute now . . .''

TWENTY-ONE

By nine o'clock a second stack of logs was in the fireplace being licked by tongues of flame, and electrically charged bug lamps were zapping insects that tried to eavesdrop on the strategy meeting being held on the veranda.

Manny Cortez painted a sad, grim picture of the situation in San Rio Blanco. It seemed that, over the past year, Malavida Valdez had been boldly expanding a criminal empire centered around the cultivation and export smuggling of high-grade marijuana grown in the fertile soil of the hillsides surrounding San Rio Blanco. There had been initial protests from the townsfolk over Valdez's activities, but he had retaliated by recruiting a ragtag army of misfits and cutthroats to enforce his will. His reign was one of terror, backed by threats and displays of violence that had brought the local populace to its knees. The citizens of San Rio Blanco, once outspoken in their denunciation of Malavida Valdez, now found themselves pressed into servitude on his behalf, rounded daily into trucks and driven to the outskirts of the village, where they worked at gunpoint to help in the harvesting of the crime czar's cash crop. Valdez had been able to keep up his brazen exploitation of the villagers for so long through his control over all forms of communication between San Rio Blanco and the outside world. A few weeks ago, however, a daring youth from the town had made his way past the guerrillas guarding the exits from San Rio Blanco and made his way to Acapulco, where he had detailed Valdez's exploits to Manny Cortez, who at the time was working with Al Massey on a story about the counterfeiting of historical artifacts by a small group of insurgents living in the run-down section of Acapulco. Both Massey and Cortez had dropped the counterfeiting story and stole their way into San Rio Blanco, where they were in the process of substantiating the charges against Valdez when Valdez had found out about them and initiated the raid that had led to Massey's disappearance. Cortez had been lucky to escape with his life and had been trying without success to convince local authorities to come to San Rio Blanco's aid since.

"I suspect Valdez is lining the pockets of those who should be helping us," Manny concluded before taking a sip of tequila to soothe the hoarseness that had begun to thicken his words.

"Well, he's not lining our pockets," Hannibal said, speaking on behalf of the A-Team. "We're here to help, so let's get down to it, shall we?"

For the first time that evening, Manny Cortez smiled. "Thank you."

"Save that for later," Hannibal said, dragging a safety match across the framework of the table they were all gathered around. The match popped, giving off a flicker of flame that Hannibal promptly applied to the end of his cigar. He looked around the table, asking his associates, "Any questions, troops?"

Amy, B.A., Murdock, and the Face Man all traded

glances with Hannibal. From the looks in their eyes, it was clear that they were all determined to carry on with the challenging task before them.

"Where do we start?" the Face Man asked.

Hannibal looked to Manny. "You said you were going to bring a map of San Rio Blanco. I think we ought to have a look at that first and take it from there."

Manny reached for the leather satchel propped against his chair and withdrew a rolled-up map. Amy and Peck cleared off the table as Manny spread out the map, an elaborate rendering of both San Rio Blanco and the surrounding hillsides. The topography was clearly defined, as were the outlines of the main buildings of the town.

"Valdez usually comes in from this direction," Manny explained, pointing to a wide valley adjacent to the main road leading up to the village. "It's all open out here, so any strategically placed sentry could spot him almost a mile and a half away."

Hannibal contemplated the map, letting a plan slowly take seed in his mind. "Manny, you have to have some idea where the marijuana fields are."

"Somewhere in this area, here." Cortez dragged a finger across a belt of hills surrounding the village. "The townspeople who have been forced to work in the fields estimate them to be approximately five miles away. That puts the fields somewhere in this radius."

"Isn't anyone able to come up with some landmarks or anything that would help us pinpoint them better?" Amy asked.

Manny shook his head. "Whenever Valdez takes them out there, they're always blindfolded. The man is mad, but he's no fool, unfortunately."

"Don't worry," Murdock interjected, "if they're inside a five-mile radius, I'll spot 'em from the air."

Analyzing the layout of the village, Hannibal pointed out a few structures and asked Manny, "How secure are these buildings?"

"Not very," Manny said. "I wouldn't use them for cover."

"Hmmmmm, we're gonna need some armor plating, Face," Hannibal said.

The Face Man was taking notes under the dull light of the bug lamp. He swatted aside a fallen moth and scribbled something on the pad.

"And a deuce and a half," B.A. put in, thinking in terms of land transport. "Maybe a dump truck. Something big."

"Ten wheeler . . ." Peck murmured as he wrote it down.

Manny passed Hannibal the tequila, and Hannibal tilted the bottle back for a long swill, then smacked his lips. "I think maybe we ought to spray that guy's field . . . bring in a crop duster with some kind of poison, just to get his dander up. I always like it when the mark is angry. They don't think straight. It will bring him to us, too, maybe. That'd be another plus, making him play in our field."

"Poisons," the Face Man jotted down. "A crop duster."

Things were starting to fall into place. Hannibal stared out at the dark sea, elaborating on the scenario. "Some heavy artillery," he thought aloud. "A three-inch gun would be nice. Recoilless, if we can get one."

The Face Man hesitated before writing it down. "That's gonna be tough to work into a movie called *Boots and Bikinis*."

"Not if it's combat boots that are going with the bikinis,"

Hannibal speculated. "Let's work on a rewrite that'll have a national guard force located just outside a beach resort. Play up the high jinks of our men in uniform when they take leave from the barracks . . . something like that."

"I don't understand this," Manny confessed. "How are you going to get all these things?"

"We're not," Hannibal informed him, grinning slyly. "Miguel Perez is."

"The film commissioner? I don't see how . . ."

"You will, my friend," Hannibal promised. "You will . . ."

The Face Man got up from the table and cracked his knuckles. "I guess I better hit the typewriter. Sounds like I got my work cut out for me. . . ."

TWENTY-TWO

The following morning the Face Man and Amy were lounging alongside the olympic-sized swimming pool located behind the villa, soaking up rays from the just-risen sun. Amy was wearing a formfitting designer swimsuit, her hair pulled back and her face glistening with a layer of Coppertone. Peck sipped a tall glass of orange juice and peered over the top of his sunglasses at Miguel Perez, who fidgeted uncomfortably in his chaise lounge, his attention torn between the listing of props Face had just given him and the reclining figure of Amy.

"Boobala," the Face Man called out, snapping his fingers to get Perez's attention. "You know I'm in trouble with Andre. I mean, chickie, my job is hanging by the ol' threadola. I need some help here . . ."

"But, Mr. Peck," Perez pleaded, "a crop duster? Three-inch metal plating? None of these things were in the script that I read . . ."

"Come on, you gotta be kidding!" Face said, feigning shock. Glancing over at his female cohort, he cried out, "Amy!"

"Yeah, yeah, so I heard," Amy said with the bored

indifference of overpaid help. She shifted on her chair and tapped the script lying on the table beside her. "It's all in the blues," she told Perez. "You did get the blue pages, didn't you?"

"Blue pages?" Perez said wonderingly. "Why, no . . ."

"You were supposed to be on the distribution list for all revisions. They came in just last night." Amy sat upright and pulled on a terry cloth bathrobe, much to Miguel's chagrin. Standing up, she went over to the phone set out on the edge of a long planter running the length of the pool. "I'll straighten that out with our people, don't worry. For now, though, I'll messenger my script out and get another copy made for you. How's that, Mr. Perez?"

"Miguel . . . call me Miguel, please," Perez said falteringly. While Amy dialed the number of the phone she was using and carried on a conversation with a busy signal, the film commissioner continued his attempt to make sense of the Face Man's prop list. "I still don't see . . . the story I read is about three American blondes who fall in love with a lifeguard, a bullfighter, and a Mexican schoolteacher. Where does this crop duster and armor plating come in?"

The Face Man pulled off his sunglasses and twirled them between his fingers, making certain that Perez could see him rolling his eyes with impatience. "Okay, Miguel, I can see that you folks apparently have a different way of making movies than we do back up in the States. Let me clue you in on a few things, okay?"

"Well, we would very much like to increase the prestige of our film industry," Perez admitted. "I am trying to be open to suggestions. Please have patience."

"It's my doctor who's going to have a patient if Andre holds me responsible for any more screw-ups, chickie,"

Peck said. "Okay, listen up . . . the first rule of Hollywood is never . . . I repeat, never question the director, especially when he's also the executive producer and the one who signs your paycheck. Now that's only logical, am I right?"

"Yes, yes, I can see that . . ."

"Good, we're halfway home then. More juice, Mike?" The Face Man refilled his glass, then held the pitcher out toward Perez. Miguel finished his drink, then put the glass out for more. Peck waited until Perez was settled back in his chair to continue. "Here's what's happening. . . . Andre has some idea about sticking in a cornball dream sequence. He wants to put Bo Derek on the wing of a biplane and spray this field her lover is standing in. What do you think of that?"

"Well . . ."

"You want my opinion, it's junk. Primo crap. That kind of trash went out with capped teeth," Peck railed. "But the bottom line is that's what Andre wants, so that's what Andre gets. Get it?"

Perez nodded feebly as Amy rejoined them, offering a bored smile. "It's all taken care of, Mr. Per . . . I mean, Miguel. You'll have a revised script by noon."

"Uh, thank you," Miguel said, referring back to his list. "And the armor plating is for what?"

"It's not armor plating, Mike," Face said, gritting his teeth with exasperation.

Amy picked up the revised script and opened it at random as she told Perez, "It's metal bulkhead for the submarine sequence."

Before Perez could say anything, the Face Man put his hand up. "I know, I know . . . 'What submarine?' you ask. Well, the lifeguard's being rewritten, too. Now he's a

Mexican sub commander. We're doing two scenes where Loni comes aboard his sub.''

"I like that change," Amy said. "A sex symbol climbs into a phallic symbol. *Très* European. It'll be like something out of Fellini. Bold, very bold.''

"But we have no submarines in the Mexican navy," Perez said.

"What's that got to do with anything?" Peck said. "Mike, this is a fluff picture. Don't listen to my assistant here. Andre's a nut bar, pure and simple. Nothing makes sense in Hollywood anymore. Just help me, here, okay? Stick with me, boobie. At least I'm not asking you for a lousy cannon . . .''

TWENTY-THREE

The reason Peck hadn't asked the film commissioner for a lousy cannon was because Hannibal remembered seeing just such a weapon on display in front of a library they'd passed on the way to the villa the previous day. The necessary papers had been forged last night while Peck was rewriting the film script, and while Perez was being hit up for a crop duster and armor plating that morning, Hannibal and B.A. had wrangled themselves a tow truck and had showed up at the library with supposed orders from the Mexican National Guard to reclaim the cannon for refurbishing and a return to use at the local base. The head librarian put up little resistance to the order, saying that she'd been trying for years to get rid of the big gun, which she felt did little to foster the cause of reading great books or putting good use to the library's facilities.

As B.A. was backing the truck into position and fastening cables around the cannon's frame, Hannibal climbed up onto the pedestal the gun was mounted on and inspected its condition.

"Barrel's plugged with concrete, B.A.," he announced. "There's a lot of pigeon crap we're going to have to scrape away, too, to get it in working order."

"You think maybe we ought to try another plan then?" B.A. asked.

"Naw. If we just leave it now, we'll draw suspicion," Hannibal said. "It'll take a lot of work, but I think we can get this animal in firing order in a couple of hours max. Better that than risk tipping our hand trying to get another one somewhere else."

"Whatever you say, Hannibal." B.A. tightened the cables, then climbed back behind the wheel of the tow truck. The head librarian stepped out onto the front steps to watch as Hannibal hopped down from the pedestal and double-checked the cables before joining B.A. inside the main cab. Hannibal waved to the woman, and she waved back, smiling.

"I can't figure her out, Hannibal," B.A. said as he started up the engine. "Hell, we don't look like we belong to Mexico's National Guard, not by a long shot."

"You saw how eager she was to get rid of this thing," Hannibal snickered. "We could have told her we were entrepreneurs underwriting a youth gang and she wouldn't have stopped us."

"Well, here goes nothin'." B.A. revved the engine, then shifted gears and took his foot off the clutch. With a fierce spinning of its rear wheels, the truck jumped forward, drawing out the slack in the cable. When the cable went taut, the cannon creaked loudly on its foundation but did not give way. B.A. kept the truck running and looked over his shoulder through the rear window of the cab. "That sucker's bolted down good, Hannibal. You sure we can't unscrew those big bolts holding it down?"

"Not a chance," Hannibal said. "They're rusted on solid. Back up and try again."

"You got it." B.A. put the truck into reverse and eased

back slowly until the rear fender bumped lightly into the poured concrete of the pedestal. He looked over at Hannibal, who gave him the signal to go ahead. A second time the truck sprang forward, tires scarring the turf noisily. The cable tightened quickly, and after only a moment's hesitation, the cannon rocked free of its mooring and toppled to the ground. B.A. activated the winch, drawing in the excess cable and hoisting the cannon up onto the truck bed.

"Good fishin', B.A.," Hannibal said, slapping his partner on the back. "When this is all over, we're going to have to take this truck out on the sea and try our luck with marlin, eh?"

"Nothin' doin', man," B.A. said, bouncing in his seat as he drove over the curb and back onto the main road leading back to the villa. "We gotta drop off that cannon and get this truck back by the time that service station opens up or we're gonna be beatin' on rocks in some prison yard. They gotta have laws against grand theft auto down here, too, you know."

"Relax, B.A.," Hannibal told him. "I told you the sign at the station said they don't open until noon today. We've got plenty of time. Besides, if they catch us and give us any flack, we'll just pay 'em off. Hell, we've hardly had to put a dent in that twenty-five thou Miss Allen fronted us."

"Yeah, but that's how much each one of us is supposed to get for all we're goin' through, Hannibal. I wanna be able to buy myself a nice house and a nice car when this is over."

"You've been talking about nice houses and nice cars for ten years, B.A.," Hannibal reminded him, smiling wryly. "Maybe if you spent less money on jewelry and those designer haircuts, you'd already have both."

As B.A. stopped at the next intersection, he glared at Hannibal and warned, "You're making me mad, man. You don't wanna be making me mad."

"You're absolutely right," Hannibal said. "Sorry, my mistake."

"And don't be makin' fun of my haircut."

"I love your haircut, B.A. I've been thinking of getting one just like it."

"Very funny, sucker."

B.A. calmed down, and they drove the rest of the way back to the villa without incident. In the back corner of the property there was a large service shed filled with tools used by the estate's grounds keepers and handymen. Murdock was there already, sorting through the assortment of tools and materials for anything the A-Team could put to use in its upcoming offensive. When B.A. honked the truck horn, Murdock opened the door to the shed and helped the other two men bring the cannon inside and disconnect it from the cables. The villa's owner had left instructions for his hired workmen to assist the A-Team in any way possible, so Hannibal gave the head grounds keeper the keys to the truck and told him to drive it back to the station.

Once the cannon was set up in firing position near one of the work benches, Murdock and Hannibal went to work on the pigeon droppings while B.A. alternated between chisels, torches, and picks to begin clearing the concrete out of the gun's wide barrel. They'd been at work on their respective tasks for close to an hour when they heard another vehicle approaching the shed, backfiring as if moving to the accompaniment of a twenty-one-gun salute. Murdock went over and peered out the large shed door. then whistled lowly as he pulled the door open.

"We either got some kids on a field trip or the weirdest looking dump truck I ever saw," he told the others.

Hannibal and B.A. looked over at the doorway as a large, rumbling school bus rolled to a sputtering stop inside the shed. The Face Man was behind the wheel, and after he killed the engine, he opened the front door and bounded out, followed by Amy.

"A bus?" B.A. grumbled, wandering over to take a closer look. "What happened to the ten-wheel truck I asked for?"

"It's the best I could do on such short notice," the Face Man said. "I'm working Miguel overtime as it is. We'll just have to make do with this clunker, that's all. We're having better luck with the armor plating and the crop duster, but the poison's a problem. Perez is trying to land a big load of bleach instead."

"Hey," Murdock suggested, "use ammonia. That stuff's terrific!"

"Good idea, Murdock." Hannibal laughed, lighting his first cigar of the day as he surveyed the meager arsenal they'd managed to assemble so far. "Okay, Miss Allen will stay here with me and B.A. until we get this popgun cleaned and loaded, then we'll head out and hope for the best. Face, you go with Murdock and hit the air with that crop duster. Try to do a drop on the field sometime around noon. You got the leaflets?"

The Face Man opened the cover of his movie script, revealing a thick stack of printed flyers. "Yep. Had to spend some of Amy's cash on these and the rewrite pages."

"I've got the receipts, and I'll reimburse you once we're back in the States," Amy said, miffed. "Let's just lay off with the petty cracks, okay? You've made your point."

"Fair enough, Miss Allen," Hannibal said. "Hey, B.A., toss Peck the keys to the limousine so they can get moving. We'll pick up Manny once we've got our end of things squared away."

B.A. was mulling over the school bus, a dissatisfied look on his face. "This lemon ain't gonna make it five miles, especially when we got hills and dirt roads to travel. Tires is worn through, needs a new ring job, probably's got squishy shocks . . ."

"B.A., there's nothing you can't fix," Hannibal told him, taking the limo keys and tossing them over to Peck. "Ol' Andre's got real faith in you, boobala."

The flattery rolled off B.A. without sinking in. He raised the engine hood and shook his head with disgust at the condition of the bus's power plant. "When this thing's trailing smoke and woofing out gaskets, ol' Andre's not gonna be so happy."

As Murdock and the Face Man left the shed, Hannibal came over to B.A. and told him, "Okay, tell you what. We'll just load up the gun and worry about cleaning it later. You put in a couple hours tinkering on this barrel of bolts and make sure it'll make it to San Rio Blanco. Once we're there, you can give it another tune-up."

"Man, this bus doesn't need a mechanic, it needs a miracle," B.A. complained.

"If anyone can do it, you can," Hannibal said.

"All right, all right." B.A. started rolling up his sleeves as he concentrated on the oil-caked engine, trying to figure out his next move. "Step aside and give the man some room."

"That's the spirit, B.A." Amy cheered him on.

As B.A. started dirtying his hands on the engine, Hannibal stepped back and looked on admiringly. "I just love it when a plan comes together."

"Seems to me the last time you said that, we ended up in trouble," Amy told him.

Hannibal nodded and blew smoke. "No, Miss Allen, if I remember correctly, we were in trouble *before* I said it, not after. There's a big difference."

"Don't matter how you slice it, Hannibal," B.A. called out over his shoulder. "We're talking trouble. This ain't gonna be no picnic."

"That's okay," Hannibal reflected. "I hate picnics . . ."

TWENTY-FOUR

B.A. was halfway through performing major surgery on the bus's engine when the side door to the service shed opened with a spine-shivering creak. Jose and Jorge had returned from Mexico City, and from the ebullient expressions on their faces, Hannibal rightly assumed that their quest for the miracle aphrodisiacs of the Orient had proven successful. Taking Hannibal beyond earshot of Amy, they boasted of their trial conquests over certain women of the night frequenting the high-rent stretch of the capitol's red-light district. Surely they would now prove to be worthy lovers of the American screen goddesses they planned to be bedding by week's end. Hannibal played up to their macho posturings, informing the two men that their roles were being beefed up and that they would now be playing a submarine commander and a crack aviator, respectively. Jorge took the bait particularly well, as Hannibal had hoped. When Hannibal said they were having trouble rounding up prop weapons for use in the rewritten scenes, the owner of the villa took the A-Team's leader to the back corner of the shed, where he unlocked a steel-plated door and ushered Hannibal into a glorified bomb shelter stocked with a number of weapons, all of them genuine and accompanied by countless rounds of ammunition.

"Take what you like," Jorge said. "My favorite is the Uzi submachine gun. Very deadly. Very light."

"Yes, I know," Hannibal said, spotting the disassembled weapon in a contour-molded suitcase. "I think we could write in a real good scene for you using that. And that Thompson's a tidy little piece of pistol, too."

"Take that, too," Jorge offered. "Everything, if you like! I keep this against the chance of revolutionaries coming to take away what is mine, but this is not the season for revolution. I have no worries for now, so take them, please. I only ask that you let Loni know it is from me that these fine weapons come, because I am a great warrior."

"You've got yourself a deal, Jorge," Hannibal said.

With Amy's assistance, the three men transferred the entire arsenal into the back of the bus, then loaded the clogged cannon. B.A. continued working around the grease and grime until he figured he'd done all he could to up the odds that the bus would make it to San Rio Blanco without breaking down. By the time he'd slammed down the engine covering and washed his hands in the cast-iron tubs by the work benches, Hannibal had sent Jose and Jorge off with the latest revisions of the film script, telling them that Bo, Loni, and Farrah would be flying down over the weekend to start rehearsals.

"Okay, let's get outta here," Hannibal said, climbing into the bus and gesturing for Amy and B.A. to do the same. He and Amy slipped into seats halfway back on the bus, whie Baracus took the wheel and adjusted the seat as best he could to conform to his driving style.

"This engine still ain't gonna purr," B.A. forewarned

Hannibal. "Sucker needs reincarnation, or at least a major overhaul."

"As long as it runs, it'll be fine with us," Hannibal told him. "Let's go, let 'er rip!"

B.A. started the engine, and the whole framework of the bus writhed with spasms as the pistons slapped noisily and tried to get their act together. A noxious blue-black cloud spewed forth from the tail pipe. The engine revved, faded, then revved again before finally settling on a high idling speed. B.A. went through the gears quickly to acquaint himself with the shifting, then put the bus into reverse and backed out of the shed.

"San Rio Blanco, here we come!" Amy said hopefully.

"Don't forget we have to pick up Manny on the way," Hannibal reminded her and B.A.

"Yeah, well he better be ready to go when we cruise by, 'cause I'm afraid if I stop this sucker it ain't gonna start again," B.A. said as he ground gears and started forward.

As they rumbled down the main road leading back into the city, the trio fell quiet, giving themselves over to private thoughts. Hannibal busied himself with inspecting their newly obtained weapons. He was well versed in the use of all of them, and Amy watched with a reflexive admiration at the smooth precision with which he handled the guns. He finally noticed her watching him and nonchalantly asked, "How's it going?"

Smiling, Amy said, "A person could get whiplash the way you guys move so fast. We barely took off from L.A. twenty-four hours ago."

Hannibal put a quick finger to his lips as he motioned in the direction of B.A. "Don't forget that we've been here longer than that as far as he's concerned."

"Oh, that's right," Amy said, lowering her voice. "Sorry. It's just that . . . well, I just want to tell you, when we were first flying down here, I really thought you guys were crazy. . . . Maybe you are and I've just gotten used to it. I don't know. Everything you do seems off-the-wall, unexpected . . . but it always ends up looking like there's been some master plan that keeps on working out in the end. Am I making any sense?"

Hannibal nodded, setting aside the Uzi in favor of the Thompson submachine gun. He polished the stock and barrel with the sleeve of his jacket as he told Amy, "Pardon my blasphemy, but, like the Lord, we work in mysterious ways."

"Exactly," Amy said, shifting in her seat as B.A. took a corner wide and then swerved back into the right lane. Speaking just loud enough to be heard over the lame thumping of the engine, she went on, "Nothing about you is as it appears . . . like when I first met Templeton Peck. I figured he was one of those real lookers with a fast line for anything with a skirt and . . . well . . ."

"And you're wondering why he hasn't hit on you?" Hannibal guessed.

"Yeah."

"Well, I'll tell you something, Miss Allen," Hannibal droned, testing the sights on the Thompson. "Unconventional though we may be, we're professionals. A client's a client, and we won't do anything that gets in the way of that particular kind of relationship."

"Well, I certainly respect you for that," Amy said, "but, you know, I can't help but wondering about what you guys are like . . . I mean, when you're not on the lam or risking your necks. Take you, for instance. Tell me about John 'Hannibal' Smith. Where do you come from?"

Hannibal let out a derisive snort. "What is this, an interview for *People* magazine?"

"I'm just curious," Amy said. "Off the record, if you like."

Hannibal eased back in his seat, setting the gun aside. He stared out the window, watching the rows of palms race by as they closed in on the city. At last he sighed and said, with an air of wistfulness, "Actually, I'm a rancher."

"A rancher?" Amy was shocked. "As in rope 'em and brand 'em?"

Hannibal nodded. "Got over two hundred acres and more head of cow than people in the nearby town can count. Ahhhhhhhhh, I sure do miss ridin' out to the north forty on a crisp Sunday morning . . . sitting on top of Ol' Topper, just lookin' out across my spread. Yessir, it's nice to have a place I call home, even if I can't be there . . ."

Amy felt her throat tightening with emotion, but then she took a hard look at Hannibal and spotted the sparkle in his eye. "You're not a rancher," she surmised, swinging her toe across the aisle and jabbing Hannibal in the shin. "That's all bull."

Hannibal looked at the young reporter, unable to keep a straight face. "Well, it's a nice thought, though, isn't it?"

"If that's what you really want out of life, I hope you're able to have it someday," Amy said. "I mean it."

"Thanks," Hannibal said. Clearing his throat, he got up from his seat and moved away from Amy, telling her, "I think I'll go tinker around with the cannon until we pick up Manny."

"What's the matter, Hannibal? Afraid to drop the tough guy act? You don't have to put on a show for me, you know. You can think of me as a friend as well as a client."

Hannibal looked back over his shoulder at Amy, holding onto the seat beside him for balance as the bus bounded along. "Let me work on that one for a while, Miss Allen."

Amy opened her mouth to say something more, but Hannibal turned his back to her and made his way to the cannon, giving it his full attention. Amy made sure he wasn't looking, then reached into her purse, snapping off the microcassette player she'd been using to record their conversation. She ejected the tape and held it in her hand a moment, staring at it with the intensity of a mystic plumbing the depths of a crystal ball. She seemed to be struggling with a decision, and finally, with some semblance of resolve, she carefully slipped the tape back into place, making sure Hannibal hadn't seen her.

"Once a reporter, always a reporter," she whispered to herself.

TWENTY-FIVE

Manny Cortez tried convincing his colleagues in the city to join him in the attempt to liberate San Rio Blanco from Malavida Valdez, but to a man, the locals frequenting the cantina balked at such a commitment, and when the battered bus limped out of Acapulco to test its mettle on the mountainous roadways, Manny was the only additional passenger.

"You've rounded up more firepower than I had thought possible," Manny told Hannibal as he eyeballed the munitions stored inside the bus. "I'm impressed."

"Yeah, well save the applause for the time being," Hannibal said. "Having weapons is one thing. Having people who can use them is another. We still have to stir a little backbone into your people in the village. Good as we are, we can't crack this gig by ourselves."

"Of course," Manny said glumly. "That will be a difficult task. My people are very frightened, and for good reason."

They fell silent and stared out the window through the raised dust of the bus's slow ascent toward San Rio Blanco. B.A. stuck to low gears, and the engine seemed perpetually on the verge of turning over for the last time.

"Too much weight in here, man," B.A. said, keeping the accelerator all the way to the floor. "I don't think we're gonna make it."

"Nonsense, B.A., you're doing fine," Hannibal called out to him.

"You won't be sayin' that when you're out pushin', sucker!"

"If it's any help," Manny suggested, "I know of some side roads that are more switchbacks than this stretch. It would take us a little longer to get there, but it would be easier on the bus."

"That's what we need, man," B.A. said.

"Go on up and navigate, Manny," Hannibal said.

A few dozen yards up the road, Manny pointed out a turn and B.A. took it. The secondary road was little more than a gravel-strewn path, and there were times when the tires of the bus extended out past the clearing and bounded roughly off the shoulder.

"I'm glad I had a light breakfast," Amy remarked as she clung to the armrest beside her.

"I just hope we don't stumble onto an enemy guard post," Hannibal said, cradling the Thompson submachine gun in his lap as he scoured the brushland surrounding the path. "I'm hoping that if there's fighting to be done, we'll be doing it on our own terms and on our own turf."

None of Valdez's men appeared, however, and finally the bus cleared the last hump of pathway and merged once more with the main road leading into San Rio Blanco. Their arrival wasn't a moment too soon, either. Hot jets of angry steam were billowing out from a leak in the radiator when B.A. brought the bus to a stop in the center of the market square, which had been put back in order since the demolition caused in the wake of Al Massey's flight from the village days before.

Manny was the first one out, and by the time the others had joined him in the square, villagers were slowly beginning to emerge from hiding, vaguely reassured by the sight of their native son. Manny waved them over as he told Hannibal, "I was born in this town. My family has lived here for two hundred years. These people are good."

"Like I was saying," Hannibal reminded him, "I hope they've got some bravery inside them, too."

"We'll find out soon enough." Manny put a call out for all those townspeople around him to return to their homes and spread word for the whole village to assemble in front of the town hall in half an hour so that they could all discuss the fate of San Rio Blanco. The noon bells were ringing from the church tower by the time Cortez's request had been carried out and several hundred worried men, women, and children huddled under the wrath of the sweltering sun to hear Manny speak. Hannibal, B.A., and Amy stood off to one side, sizing up the audience's reaction as Manny stressed the need for his people to take a stand against Malavida Valdez.

The first response came from a middle-aged man whose floppy, wide-brimmed hat did little to hide the bruises and welts on his face. "No!" he lamented, his voice racked with pain as he exhorted the masses. "How many more of you want to be beaten by that maniac or those pigs who ride with him?"

This brought about a widespread murmuring, over which Manny shouted insistently, "If you don't fight back, he'll continue to beat you! How long can this go on?"

Another man broke away from the crowd and raised his voice to be heard. "He is right! Our fathers would spit on us. We have been cowards. It is better to fight and die than to run like children!''

Anxious to build some momentum based on the man's shouted sentiment, Hannibal stepped forward and said, ''We are here because we are friends of Al Massey. You know who he is. He tried to help you himself before he disappeared.''

The man who had first spoken out against any form of resistance protested once more, climbing onto a nearby step to make himself more visible. ''He was dragged from this town by Malavida Valdez! The same fate awaits those who dare speak of defiance! I, for one, do not wish to fight. We are not soldiers!''

''I'm a soldier,'' Hannibal told him evenly, shouting the words with a fierce pride so that they filled the air. ''I can show you how to fight.''

The man with the hat shook his head miserably and cried out, ''It's no use. We are not strong enough to win against Valdez.''

''Hey!'' B.A. roared angrily, moving next to Hannibal and pointing a finger at the complainer. ''What you sayin', turkey?'' When the other man withered back into the anonymity of the crowd, B.A. lectured the whole group, pacing to keep his anger under control. ''You gonna let this Valdez jerk keep beatin' on your heads forever?

''There ain't nothin' in this world worth losin' your pride for. Life don't mean nothin' unless you can hold your head high. I come from a place where the rats is big as alley cats. I got no money and no house, but ain't nobody ever messed in my mud.'' B.A. glared at the townsfolk, and he could see he was having an effect, so he kept driving his point home. ''Look at you . . . standing there lookin' at your shoes, moanin' about this fat, dumb bandit. . . . I suppose I can understand one man runnin' scared . . . but a whole town? A whole village? You people might as well be dead.''

B.A. turned his back on the populace and walked into the shadows of the town hall. The people of San Rio Blanco slowly absorbed the tongue-lashing they'd just received, and an uncomfortable silence filled the town square. Manny Cortez gave them time to think, then exclaimed, ''I call for a vote. All those who would drive this bandit Valdez from our town, raise their hands. . . .''

After a moment's hesitation, a few arms shot upright from amidst the throng. As Manny began to count hands, the numbers slowly began to multiply, buoyed up by verbal cries of support. Newly instilled courage swept over the people, and while a few villagers meekly broke away and retreated, the vast majority eventually had their hands thrust in the air as they continued to spur themselves on with shouts and cries of support.

''We can do it!''

''We can drive him out!''

''It is time we became men!''

''Down with Valdez!''

''We will make our town safe for our children once again!''

Hannibal observed the rallying masses, then looked over at B.A. and cried out, ''I'd say you've got a bright future in politics, Baracus!''

''Nothin' doin','' B.A. said, struggling to hold back a grin of satisfaction. ''I just like to give folks a swift kick when they need one, that's all.''

''Well, I'd say you just did some nice kicking, then,'' Hannibal said. ''Now, let's see what we can do about turning all this enthusiasm into action. . . .''

With Manny acting as a liaison, the A-Team began coordinating the countless preparations needed for the planned overthrow of Malavida Valdez. The strongest men of the village were sent over to the rear of the bus. Half of them helped in the unloading of the munitions and armor plating from the back of the bus. As the weaponry was being carried off to the market square for distribution and lessons in handling, the other men put their bulk to use in pushing the bus into the nearest service station so that B.A. could attempt a second resuscitation of the fragile vehicle. A handful of men busied themselves with unclogging the cannon and lubricating all the necessary moving parts to make it operable again. Hannibal took a tour of the town, committing its layout to memory as he plotted the best way to arrange for an effective defense against the anticipated arrival of Valdez's rebel force.

The children of the village took a liking to B.A., and as he went about his duties, he found an ever-present group of youths tagging along beside him, watching his every move. He warned them to stay clear when he was busy using a welding torch to cut the armor plating into small, contoured sheets, but once he settled down to working on the engine of the bus, he let them crowd near him once more. When Amy stopped by to check on him, she found B.A. patiently explaining his mechanical prowess as he took wrenches from the children and put them to use on the engine.

"Got yourself some help, huh?" she said with a smile as she came over to where he was working.

"I like kids," B.A. confessed.

"And they seem to like you, too," Amy noted. "I guess they're not fooled by that habitual scowl you're always wearing. Is that your protective shield or something?"

B.A. wrestled a lug nut loose, then wiped sweat from his brow as he looked up at Amy. "The way I am is the way I am," he asserted. "If I scare people . . . well, it gives me room."

"But how can you work with people . . . how can they work with you if they're afraid you'll rip their tongues out if they say the wrong thing to you?"

B.A. laughed and handed his wrench to one of the kids, then picked up a screwdriver from another. "You talkin' about Hannibal?" he asked Amy. "He ain't afraid of me. He ain't afraid of nothin'!"

"Does he have some kind of death wish?"

"Naw, he's just got the jazz, that's all," B.A. said as he tinkered with the carburetor. "Hannibal's got the jazz."

"The jazz?"

"He's been livin' on the edge since I known him," B.A. explained. "He's one crazy hooked-together dude. You never know where he's gonna come from or how he's gonna move on ya. That's what kept him alive through Nam. Kept me an' the others alive, too."

B.A. finished adjusting the carburetor, then looked over the assortment of tools the kids were holding out to him. He took the spark plug wrench and put it to use, humming contentedly to himself. The children tried to hum along and giggled when they strayed from the song he was humming.

"Why do you do it?" Amy asked. "All this wild stuff with the A-Team? I'm sure you could find safer ways to live outside the law until your name is cleared."

"Just like Hannibal, I do it for the jazz," B.A. admitted. He checked the gap on one of the spark plugs, then another. "It's like walkin' into a casino in Vegas, layin' down your bucks, and hittin' on the first roll. You can't walk away. You just can't. You know you can beat 'em. You know it, 'cause you done it.''

"That's not the same thing as this, though," Amy said.

"Sure it is," B.A. insisted. "You'll see. If you want this guy Valdez bad enough, an' we get 'im, you'll feel it. Wait an' see. Just wait an' see. . . ."

TWENTY-SIX

Howling Mad Murdock wasn't vocally equipped to pose any threat to Pavarotti or Domingo, but that didn't stop him from treating the Mexican countryside to a sampling of operatic favorites as he navigated a cherry-red biplane through the heat of the afternoon. His faulty tenor straddled most notes and stumbled over others, but he continued to sing loudly and with full fervor, ecstatic at the chance to be at the controls of the vintage warplane, which Miguel Perez had procured from an eccentric industrialist who lived on the coast and was glad to be a part of any motion picture starring Bo Derek. The Face Man had promised the plane's owner a dozen signed photos of Bo poised on the plane's wing prior to the shooting of the scene in which she performed her climactic stunt. The photos *had* been taken just before the plane had set out for San Rio Blanco, but the person on the wing hadn't been Bo Derek, but rather Templeton Peck, wearing World War I aviator goggles and a matching leather cap that further obscured his features. Now Peck was riding in the forward cockpit, telling himself over and over that Howling Mad Murdock was not really crazy.

"He knows what he's doing," the Face Man chanted as he braced himself for another barrel roll. "He knows what he's doing. He's a crack aviator, as sane as can be."

"*A te o cara!*" Murdock suddenly began to wail above the drone of the plane's engine, launching into a bastardized stream of Bellini arias.

"He's not really crazy," Peck whispered, "he's not crazy."

Murdock opened the throttle and swung the nose of the biplane upward, singing at the top of his lungs as he negotiated a full loop. Tanned as he was, Peck's face still turned white as the plane reached the top of the loop, flying upside down so that there was only air between him and a thousand-foot fall to the ground. His heart lunged to his throat, and he was contemplating prayer when Murdock brought the plane out of its loop and began to right their course toward the sloping hills surrounding San Rio Blanco.

"What have I ever done to you, Murdock?" the Face Man yelled over his shoulder.

"Hey, man, this is a blast, don'tcha think?" Murdock shouted back happily, as if he hadn't heard Peck. "It's like Disneyland, only you can stay on the same ride as many times as you want. Isn't that great?"

"Do they have barf bags on this plane?" the Face Man wanted to know.

Murdock grinned like a maniac, then started in on a verse from *La Sonnambula* as he skimmed above the nearby treetops. He was gearing up for another series of barrel rolls when he suddenly stopped singing. When Peck looked back to thank Murdock, Howling Mad pointed down at the ground below. The Face Man glanced down, and his eyes widened at the sight of a rolling field of marijuana plants. There must have been several hundred of the thick bushes, each one as tall as a man. A handful of armed desperadoes patrolled the perimeter of the field. Half of them looked up at the antique biplane and quickly unslung their rifles while the other half started running for higher ground, where they thought they might be able to get off better shots.

"No more stalling, Rickenbacker," the Face Man told Murdock. "This here's Operation Hit and Run. I don't want this bird air-conditioned any more than it already is."

Murdock circled about as tightly as possible, then bore down on the fields from another angle, flying a slight zigzag pattern to make them a less easy target to hit.

"Okay, that's it," the Face Man said, giving Murdock a hand signal. "Hit 'em with the ammonia. Now!"

Howling Mad tugged on a lever at his side, emptying a tankload of undiluted ammonia through spray nozzles suspended beneath the plane. A pungent, burning mist descended upon the marijuana crop like a fast-moving fog. There was a guerrilla in the path of the downpour, and as he was raising his rifle for a potshot at the passing biplane, he suddenly let out an agonized scream from the stinging assault of the ammonia. In their own way, the surrounding plants were letting out silent cries of anguish.

"Che gelida manina!" Murdock sang the role of Rodolfo in La Bohème with stirring passion as he banked the plane sharply to one side, averting contact with a spray of lead coming from the guns of the other guards.

"Good thing Bo isn't out on the wing now," the Face Man exclaimed as he readied himself for their second approach over the marijuana fields. He'd overcome his initial reservations and was now feeling what B. A. Baracus so affectionately referred to as "the jazz." Matching Murdock's manic grin with one of his own, Peck reached inside his jacket and pulled out the printed flyers he'd made up earlier. In large, bold letters, the pamphlets read: "COURTESY OF THE TOWN OF SAN RIO BLANCO."

"Bombs away!" As Murdock was releasing the second tankful of ammonia onto another section of the fields, the Face Man tossed the pamphlets out of the plane. They separated immediately and fluttered like birds with broken wings to the ground, landing amidst the ruined crops. By the time any of the guards could reach the flyers and learn who was behind the aerial bombardment, Murdock was guiding the biplane away from the fields and toward San Rio Blanco.

"Figaro!" the Face Man sang boldly, making his contribution to the afternoon's recital. "Figaro Figaro Fiiiiiiiig-arooooooooooo!!!!"

The touring opera company continued to fill the air with song all the way to the mountain village, where Murdock flew low, dodging steeples and telephone poles as he gave the Face Man a kingfisher's view of the main road. Cries went up from the people of San Rio Blanco as they waved their greetings to the two men in the biplane. By now they'd already been told of the act by which the A-Team hoped to provoke Valdez into action, and they assumed that the boisterous arrival of Murdock and the Face Man indicated that their mission had been a success.

There was an expansive clearing between the town hall and the marketplace, and Murdock chose it as the best place around to land the biplane. Cutting the engines as he touched down, the eccentric aviator used a combination of fancy steering and brake-pumping to bring the plane to a stop a few yards shy of a concrete wall encircling the town hall. Riding in front, the Face Man waited until they were no longer moving before he dared to open his eyes. Seeing how close they'd come to a bona fide crash landing, he let out a long breath, then turned and told Murdock, "Tidy, my friend. Very tidy."

"Too bad I was running low on fuel," Murdock quipped. "I was looking forward to belting out 'O muto asil.' It would have rounded out things perfectly, wouldn't you say?"

"Perhaps another time, Murdock."

Fifty yards from where the biplane had landed, the doors to a small barn swung open and B.A. jogged out along with Hannibal. Between them they were carrying a .50 caliber machine gun of roughly the same vintage as the plane. Amy brought up the rear.

"Came off without a hitch," the Face Man told the others once they reached the plane. When he noticed B.A. and Hannibal hoisting the machine gun onto the frame of the plane, just above the engine, he said, "Hey, what gives?"

"Control the air and you win the war," Hannibal reminded him.

"But won't we shoot the prop off?" the Face Man said warily.

B.A. pulled a length of shining chain out of his pocket and waved it in Peck's face, explaining, "That's what this is for, man. Timing chain . . . gun fires through the blades of the prop."

Peck couldn't believe what he was hearing. He cocked his head and looked back at the pilot one more time. "Is he nuts, Murdock?"

"No, I'm nuts, remember." Murdock snickered. "B.A.'s just an angry mudsucker."

"Hey, keep it up, Murdock, and I'll teach you how to fly without a plane," B.A. warned.

"There's doctors at the hospital with funny pills that already taught me that," Murdock countered.

"Hey, you guys, lay off it, would you?" Hannibal growled, trying to concentrate on mounting the gun. "Are we the A-Team or a Cub Scout pack?"

Amy let out a short laugh, amused at the men's constant squabbling. "I'll tell you one thing, I'm sure not a den mother. . . ."

TWENTY-SEVEN

It was late in the afternoon when Malavida Valdez headed up the caravan of cutthroats returning to San Rio Blanco. They rolled into town much the same way as they had when they'd come for Al Massey, and they found the reception to be equally cold. The streets were once again vacant, and today there was not even a wind to stir up dust. The bells in the church tower tolled morosely, and the animals of the village put out their barnyard chorus as the intruders waited impatiently for the appearance of those who had dared to violate the fields of Valdez.

"You think you can spit on me?!!" Valdez roared, climbing down from his jeep and addressing the unseen townsfolk. "I will have your stinking lives for this! You cannot hide . . . not from Malavida Valdez!!"

As before Valdez motioned for Paco to give the people something to think about. The burly subordinate eased his bulk out of the next jeep and raised his automatic rifle, drawing bead on the church tower. Applying slight pressure on the trigger, Paco sent a rapid volley ramming into the much-abused bells. The discordant peal carried on for long seconds after the man had ceased firing, and Malavida let loose with chilling laughter, anticipating the timid reappearance of Enrique Salizon, the town's mayor, to beg for mercy. What he got instead was a burst of return fire from the vicinity of the tower. Bullets nipped at the dirt around Valdez's feet, forcing him to do an awkward dance to avoid losing his toes. The gunfire persisted, moving away from the rebel leader and feasting on the grillwork of the nearest jeep. Water gushed outward from the radiator's wounds, and the jeep pitched forward at a sharp angle when one of the front tires was french-kissed by hot lead. Valdez's men scrambled for cover, crying out with surprise at this latest show of insolence.

Once he'd spent a full clip of ammunition, Hannibal moved away from his cover in the bell tower and shouted out to Valdez, "Hey, fatso, up here!"

Valdez peered up from the rear of his jeep, where he'd dived for protection. Spotting Hannibal, he yelled back, "Hey, muchacho, why you shoot at Malavida?"

"Because you're a rotten piece of crud," Hannibal told him as he slipped another ammo clip into the Thompson. "You oughta be hung by your heels in a vat of pig slop!"

"You're gonna make me angry, gringo," Valdez threatened as he reached behind his back, trying to signal one of his men to take a shot at Hannibal.

"You ain't smart enough to get angry," Hannibal retorted, edging back behind the framework of the bell tower. "You're just mean and stupid."

Valdez looked over his shoulder to see what was holding up his sharpshooters. There were half a dozen of them taking up various strategic positions around the convoy of jeeps, but none of them were able to get Hannibal in the sights of their rifles. Trying to hide his frustration, Valdez tried bluffing.

"You talk big, gringo, but you are one man alone in a bell tower. You have the high position, but you are alone. Maybe I take a grenade and blow your house down." Valdez laughed again, like the big, bad wolf.

"You're even more stupid than I guessed. What makes you think I'm alone?" Hannibal pulled his head back as a few rifle shots gouged the stucco and two of the smaller bells. One bullet ricocheted against the inner wall of the tower and ripped through the loose sleeve of Hannibal's shirt, barely missing his flesh. Hannibal inspected the hole, then reached for a walkie-talkie on the ledge beside him and barked into the mouthpiece, "Give this gonzo a haircut."

Howling Mad Murdock was on the receiving end of the message, manning the controls of the refuelled biplane. He'd been flying the aircraft in a holding pattern outside of town, but once Hannibal gave the green light, he gave Peck the thumbs up signal and abruptly changed course. Moments later the red-winged fighter was roaring through the heart of the village, bearing down on the bandits as if with kamikaze intent. Valdez and his sharpshooters all hit the dirt as the plane zoomed overhead. Peck had his hands on the plane's big gun, but he held back from demonstrating their firepower capabilities for the time being. Murdock brought the plane back up as they cleared the main street, then started flying lazy eights within view of the guerrillas.

Valdez watched the plane a few seconds, then looked around the town, wondering how many other troops might be hidden there. When no one else showed themselves, however, his confidence returned, and he decided to try luring Hannibal out into the open so he could put this resistance down as quickly as possible.

"Señor, you make a big mistake with me," he called up

to Hannibal. "There is no need for us to be enemies. This town is full of men with no heart. You and I, maybe we make a deal. Maybe you come down from there and we talk."

"Give me a break, Valdez. You think I'm one of your brainless goons?" Hannibal shouted scornfully. "Here's the deal. . . . You give me Al Massey, then turn your jeeps around and get out of town, for good."

"And if I say no?" Valdez countered.

"Then I turn you into a taco dinner," Hannibal threatened. "You got thirty seconds, meathead, then we start blasting."

Valdez eyed the plane once more, then scanned the deserted village, calculating his chances. He finally decided that Hannibal was bluffing. "No deal, señor," he screamed, spitting in the dirt. With the wave of his hand he ordered his men to fire.

A dozen guns emptied their ammunition into the top of the church tower, forcing Hannibal to hit the floor and cover his head against the chances of being hit by the bullets and stray shrapnel that flew about the ringing enclosure like lethal mosquitoes.

While the bandits were absorbed with trying to demolish the tower, the next phase of the A-Team's offensive swung into action. Across the market square the frail door of the service station exploded open as the recreated bus lunged into daylight. No longer a meager transporter of schoolchildren, the bus had been layered with sheets of armor plating and painted black so that it looked like a wheelbound cross between the *Monitor*, the *Merrimac*, and some scaly black dragon. The engine was still running ragged, but the pistons put out enough power to drag the monstrous shell across the dusty road toward the enemy. All the windows, including the front windshield, were covered with the thick plating, and B.A. peered through small slits as he steered the vehicle. The reconditioned cannon had been mounted on the roof and sheathed in its own protective housing so that Manny Cortez could fire it without exposing himself. The three-inch barrel spat forth a shell that exploded into the engine compartment of one of the enemy jeeps, turning the vehicle into scrap metal and hurling its dazed occupants in all directions. Elsewhere inside the bus, other residents of San Rio Blanco poked more conventional rifles through other slats and kept the bandits on the defensive.

When the gunfire stopped banging about the belfry, Hannibal got up from the floor and dusted himself off. "Still in one piece," he assured himself. "So far so good." Taking his submachine gun with him, he went to the back side of the tower and climbed out. A lashed wooden ladder reached up to the ledge from the ground, and once he gained a footing on the first rung, he quickly descended to the ground, where he braved the war zone of the main street and made his way toward the armed bus. He had a chance to do his own share of bullet dancing by the time he reached the bus and slipped in through the rear door that Amy had hastily opened.

"Do you have the jazz yet?" she asked him with a smirk as she helped him aboard.

"Almost." Hannibal laughed, making his way past the rifle-toting villagers to the cannon, which Manny had just finished reloading. "Mind if I cut in?" Hannibal asked, stepping onto the makeshift platform affording a view through the sights of the cannon.

"Help yourself," Manny told him, moving aside.

Hannibal pivoted the cannon until he lined up a clear

shot on one of the jeeps that was turning around in the market square. He fired off a shot, and the entire bus shook with the force of the recoil. His aim was true, though, and the front left wheel of the fleeing jeep blew apart, sending the vehicle careening into the thick wall surrounding the town hall. Those aboard the jeep flew free and tumbled into the dirt, then staggered to their feet and rushed to leap aboard another transport on its way out of town.

"*Now* I've got the jazz," Hannibal told Amy. Shouting to the front of the bus, he went on, "Okay, B.A., stay on 'em while we got 'em on the run!"

As the black bus continued to give chase to the fleeing rebels, the other people of the village rushed out from the cover of their homes, cheering at the valiant stand the A-Team had made on their behalf. Granted, the center of the town was bullet-riddled and trashed again, but it now seemed that there would be no further violence in San Rio Blanco. Malavida Valdez was on the run, and he was running scared. There would be much to celebrate this evening, the townsfolk told themselves happily.

The war was far from over, however.

As the chase made its way into the hills, the jeeps took advantage of their lighter weight and easier maneuverability to gain distance on the pursuing bus. By the time Hannibal had reloaded the cannon and sent off another shot, Valdez's caravan was far enough ahead that the shell dug out a crater yards shy of the last jeep.

"Haha!" Valdez howled back, "Come and get us, if you can! You are the tortoise trapped in your shell, while we are fast like the hare, and you can be sure we will not stop to rest so you can catch up with us. We live to fight another day, gringo!"

Valdez's hopes proved to be as premature as those of the citizens of San Rio Blanco, because just as the jeeps were pulling well ahead of the bus, the red biplane swooped down from the treetops to take up the chase, and the Face Man rained a shower of .50 caliber bullets down on Valdez's men. The driver of Valdez's jeep jerked the steering wheel sharply to avoid rolling into the line of fire, and Valdez, who had been standing up to voice his taunts at the bus, was thrown clear of the vehicle. He landed roughly in a thicket and swore loudly as he worked his way free. On his way back to the jeep, he waved an angry fist at the biplane.

"You will pay dearly for that, gringos!" he vowed.

Murdock was too busy singing operatic encores to notice, much less care about Valdez's displeasure. He circled the plane around and headed in from the other direction while the Face Man readied the gun for another outburst. Neither of them was able to hear the faint metallic creaking as the timing chain connecting the gun to the engine slipped a notch. It was only when the Face Man cut loose the next round that he began to suspect something was wrong.

"Hey, did you hear that pinging sound when I fired?" he shouted back at Murdock.

Murdock had heard the noise above his singing, but didn't seem overly concerned about it. "Timing chain's off just a hair," he guessed. "Bullets must be nicking the prop a little, that's all."

"That's all?" the Face Man gasped. "We only got one prop as it is, Murdock. We can't go shooting the damn thing off!"

Murdock shrugged his shoulders as he started in for another run on the jeeps. "Gotta go with the flow, baby. Hang on, here we go again!"

"Where's my Saint Christopher's medal when I need it?" the Face Man wondered dismally, gritting his teeth as he grabbed ahold of the gun and fired another round through the propeller. The pinging grew louder, but enough bullets were dodging the prop to cause damage on the ground. Whether by accident or design, Murdock and Peck had succeeded in herding the jeep convoy into a box canyon offering no avenue of escape. The jeeps ground to a halt, forming a rough circle like a wagon train making its last stand against overwhelming odds. When the armor-plated bus caught up with them, the bandits wasted a few more rounds of rifle fire trying to pierce the other vehicle's exterior, then realized the futility of it all. After Hannibal decimated another of the jeeps with a blast from the cannon, Valdez's men were ready to surrender. They threw down their rifles and stepped clear of cover.

Hannibal threw open the crude hatch covering the cannon and surfaced, puffing on a fat victory cigar as he kept his submachine gun trained on Valdez, who had yet to give up his gun. "You're outta dirt road and good luck, hombre," Hannibal told him. "Now let's have your guns down and your hands up, okay? Make it easier on all of us."

While Valdez pondered this seeming end to his short-lived dominance over San Rio Blanco, Hannibal glanced up at the biplane, where both Murdock and the Face Man were waving triumphantly from their respective cockpits.

"Well done, Murdock!" the Face Man yelled to his partner. "They'll make you an ace for this."

"How nice. Everyone always said I was a card." Murdock jockeyed the controls to fly up over the top edge of the precipice that had proved to be Valdez's dead end. He was about to indulge in another aria when he suddenly let out a low, dispirited whistle. Leaning forward, he tapped the Face Man on the shoulder and pointed down. Peck peered over the side of the plane and gaped with horror.

Approaching the cliff top overlooking the canyon where Valdez had been supposedly apprehended was a large armed force. There were several tanks, half a dozen ten-wheel troop transports, and at least twenty more jeeps, all filled with soldiers. More men walked in a column adjacent to the vehicles.

"What the hell . . . ?" Murdock exclaimed, snatching up his walkie-talkie.

"Who are those guys?" the Face Man wondered, his stomach knotting with fear.

"Hannibal," Murdock shouted into the walkie-talkie. "Ridge above you. You got company galore. If they're unfriendlies, we're in trouble."

From his perch atop the bus, Hannibal looked up and the cigar sagged between his teeth as he saw the arriving army spread out along the edge of the ridgetop. When a number of three-inch guns were lined up and pointed down at the black bus, Hannibal quickly deduced whose side the force was on. Ducking inside the bus and closing the hatch, he called out to B.A., "About face, Baracus, and step on it!"

"What's happening?" Amy asked worriedly as B.A. wrestled with the steering wheel, trying to turn the bus around.

"Seems like we wandered into a slight predicament," Hannibal understated. As if to emphasize the gravity of the situation, a pair of armor-piercing shells ploughed into the ground on either side of the bus, spitting up enough dirt and stray stone to make it sound like hail was pummeling the vehicle. The villagers inside the bus moaned and wailed fearfully as B.A. floored the accelerator and started backtracking the way they'd just traveled.

"We gotta do something!" the Face Man shouted up in the plane. "Those guns are going to eat the bus for lunch, otherwise."

"Get that stinger ready," Murdock said, cutting the plane's engines and diving toward the army below. "We're going to have to make a nuisance of ourselves and hope for the best."

The biplane angled down toward the armored division, and the Face Man clamped his finger down on the mounted gun's trigger. Bullets sprang forth with fierce intensity, but the timing chain had slipped so far out of sync that most of the shots slammed into the propeller, literally disintegrating it before Peck's eyes.

"Good-bye, sweet prince," the Face Man groaned as the plane began to lose altitude at an alarming rate. Behind him, Murdock was a picture of grim determination, working his hands with desperate speed over the controls, doing all he could to keep the plane aloft while he sought out a place to land. He narrowly averted a collision with a grove of wide-limbed oaks, then spotted a narrow cornfield just off to the right.

"Aw, shucks," he yelled as he dipped the plane down further and then leveled off. With a prolonged and vicious rustling, the aircraft touched down, pushing through the tall stalks, gradually losing speed. At last the plane stopped. Murdock and Peck looked to one another. Assured that they were unharmed, they bounded out of the cockpits and dropped to the ground, quickly losing themselves in the corn.

A mile away, the bus was faring poorly. B.A. tried to pick up speed, but the upward slope was too much for the weighty vehicle to overcome, and the bombfire from the ridgetops drew closer to them until one shot finally nicked the bus hard enough to send it tumbling onto its side into a ravine just off the side of the road. Inside, the occupants bounded off the sides and each other like popping kernels of corn. When the bus stopped moving, they picked themselves up, dazed and confused.

"You okay?" B.A. asked Amy as he helped her to her feet.

"Yeah," Amy said, nodding. "Yeah, I'm fine."

The others also seemed to have survived the crash without any severe injuries. Hannibal crawled over to his fallen walkie-talkie and spoke into it. "Face Man! You there? Murdock? Get help! They've got us!"

There was no answer from the aviators, but soon there came a rapid-fire drumming on the sides of the bus. Apparently Valdez's men had decided against surrender and had caught up with the bus.

"Come out, señor!" Valdez hounded Hannibal with uplifted spirits. "Come out and see what I have for you now!"

B.A. looked over at Hannibal. "We got no more tricks up our sleeves, man."

Hannibal nodded drearily, then reached over and grabbed a white rag from a toppled box near the cannon. Going over to the front door of the bus, he opened it and stuck his hand out, waving the rag. When he felt sure that no one was going to perforate him, he pulled himself out of the opening and offered the best smile he could muster under the circumstances. Seeing the armed reinforcements beginning to wind their way down from the ridgetop to join the bandits, Hannibal told Valdez gaily, "You sure know how to throw a party, neighbor!"

TWENTY-EIGHT

Less than a mile away from the point where the black bus had met its unfortunate fate, the vehicle's occupants found themselves being driven into a military outpost that looked to be a decade past its prime. The fortifications were weathered and crumbling in spots, and the scattered barracks were afflicted by leprous scabs of flaking paint. Appearances aside, however, the compound provided for the needs of a military force capable of posing a serious threat to the stability of not only San Rio Blanco, but to the entire region. Valdez had managed somehow to link up with an insurgent army, and it seemed only a matter of time before he would branch out his operations from mere cultivation of marijuana to all-out revolution. The A-Team had stumbled from the proverbial frying pan into a seeming fire of insurrection.

"I'm beginning to see why Massey wasn't welcome around here," Hannibal said, jostling in the back of the jeep where he had been placed after being hand-tied. Amy, B.A., and Manny Cortez were riding with him, while the other prisoners rode in the back of the jeep ahead of them.

"I just hope he's okay," Amy said.

"I hope the same," Manny added, although there was little trace of hope in his voice.

As the other transports veered off and headed in the vicinity of the barracks, the two jeeps carrying prisoners continued toward a back corner of the compound, finally coming to a stop near a section of lashed poles forming an imposing wall against intrusion from any outside force. Thick clumps of bushes were scattered about the inside grounds, and Hannibal could make out the wood and bamboo frameworks of crude cells rising above the shrubline. B.A. noticed them, too, and grumbled, "Hey, those look like the same kind of hellholes the Cong used in Nam."

"I guess we're in for a little déjà vu, then," Hannibal surmised as the soldiers riding in the front of the jeeps got out and gestured with the tips of their rifles for the prisoners to debark as well. As the prisoners were being led to the cells, the jeep carrying Valdez sped over and the rebel leader hopped out, still euphoric about the latest turn of events.

"You want Meester Massey, yes?" Valdez leered mockingly as Amy, Manny, and Baracus were shoved into the first of the cells. "He no look so good today . . ."

There was already someone inside the cell, a frail, beaten man who could stir only slightly in response to the commotion around him. Amy recognized him immediately and let out a frightened gasp as she rushed to his side.

"Al . . . Oh, Al!" Crouching down, she cradled his head in her lap and cringed at the sight of his many bruises. Massey groaned, peering up at her through his swollen eyes. "It's Amy, Al. What have they done to you?"

"A . . . Amy?" Massey grimaced as he shifted his head

for a better look at his fellow reporter. "Amy, what . . . how did you . . . I've been here for so long—"

"She come to rescue you, Massey." Valdez laughed. "They all come to rescue you. I think you should hire some better peoples next time, no?"

Hannibal scowled at Valdez and started into the cell, but one of the soldiers held him back.

"No, not you, gringo," Valdez told him. "We have some talking to do."

"Want to find out my name, rank, and serial number, is that it?" Hannibal cracked.

"We will see." Valdez sniggered.

Hannibal was led across the compound at gunpoint to a large canvas tent that was easily the newest and best-maintained structure in the camp. Inside, a bearded soldier in clean fatigues sat at a folding table, sipping whiskey as he contemplated a map of the region. He could have fared well in a Fidel Castro look-alike contest, save for the fact that his eyes held a look more of lazy arrogance than fiery determination. When Hannibal was brought in and shoved into a chair across from him, the bearded man looked up at him and grinned wryly.

"I am Colonel Flores," he said, "and you must be the man who has been causing Señor Valdez so much trouble."

"It doesn't take much to cause him trouble," Hannibal remarked, casting a sidelong glance at Valdez, who was hovering nearby like a prideful fisherman showing off the marlin he'd just caught at sea. "He keeps tripping over his I.Q."

The smile faded from Valdez's face, and he spat on the ground at Hannibal's feet. "And who is captured?" he mocked. "Who is the man about to die?"

"Don't book that one yet, scumbag," Hannibal snapped back. "And you shouldn't be dirtying up the nice colonel's floor, either. Were you brought up in a barn?"

Valdez snapped his fingers, and one of his men stepped forward, slapping Hannibal across the face. Hannibal jerked his head to one side, rolling with the blow, but he still came up with red welts across his cheek. It didn't stop him from grinning like a man with no problems in the world.

Flores took another sip of his whiskey, then sighed, idly tapping a pencil on the edge of his table. "My guess is you don't know what's going on here, anyway," he deduced. "You've been a pest, but it takes more than the likes of you to pose a threat to our operations."

"Oh, I think I've got your game plan down, Colonel," Hannibal said. "Malavida, here, he's the tax man. He's been running around, shaking down little mountain villages like San Rio Blanco, making them grow his marijuana so he can sell it to U.S. importers. He gets a fair cut and drops the rest of the money in your lap. . . . How am I doing so far?"

Colonel Flores glared hostilely at Valdez, who took a step back and swallowed hard, shaking his head. "I tell him nothing . . ."

"He's right, Colonel. I just took a lucky guess. I'm a terror on the game show circuit," Hannibal said. "Now, moving right along, with the money you bring in off the smuggling operation, you've been pumping up your army and your ego, buying secondhand weapons, tanks, half-tracks . . . While you hide out, plotting to overthrow the universe, you have your flunkies run your ragtag troops through maneuvers and hope they'll amount to something."

"You have a very irritating manner, señor," Flores said coolly, shifting the pencil from hand to hand.

"Yeah, I know," Hannibal admitted. "I've been working on my personality . . . read Don Rickles's book and everything. Nothing seems to be helping."

"I can help you with a bullet through the brain, gringo," Valdez sneered.

"Valdez . . ." Once he had the rebel's attention, Colonel Flores pointed to the doorway. Valdez hesitated, then gave Flores a perfunctory salute and left the tent. The guards stayed behind, keeping an eye on Hannibal.

"How many people know about it?" Flores asked Hannibal. "About us?"

"Hey, pal, if I were you, I'd pull out the camouflage netting," Hannibal told him. "It's in the paper in Acapulco. Manny Cortez, he works for the same newspaper syndicate Al Massey's with. Amy Allen is with the L.A. *Courier*, and she's sent off the lowdown on you, too. Then there's me and B.A. and the two guys in the crop duster. They're probably tapping out a message on the telegraph right now. I'd say you've got a serious public relations problem here."

"And I'd say you're a dead man," Flores countered.

Hannibal wasn't intimidated. "It's been tried before, ace. Besides, I'm just a pest, remember? Your real trouble's yet to come."

"What are you talking about?"

"Right now, the Mexican Army's on its way up here," Hannibal bluffed. "You better dig your cannons out of the mud, 'cause you're running out of time."

Flores set down the pencil and finished off his drink, trying to keep a poker face. He finally snickered and shook his head. "The Mexican Army? I think not, señor . . ."

TWENTY-NINE

The guerrillas who had attempted to apprehend the Face Man and Howling Mad Murdock gave up their search after combing the cornfield and slogging through the mountain stream that the errant aviators had fled down to avoid leaving tracks. Within an hour after they had disembarked from their downed plane, Peck and Murdock were coming up on the estate of the Princess Hotel's owner. They were drenched with sweat and creek water, gasping for breath, and bleeding from superficial cuts and leech hickeys. But they were still alive . . . and free.

"Some escape, eh, Murdock?" the Face Man said as they pushed through a belt of shrubs and started across the neatly trimmed lawn surrounding the villa.

"Sí," Murdock said, "it'll put my memoirs in the six-figure range, no question about it."

"I think I'll wait for the movie," Peck laughed. "I can see it now . . . 'John Travolta and Richard Gere are Howling Mad Murdock and Templeton Peck in—' "

"Shhhhh," Murdock suddenly hissed, bringing a finger to his lips and sidestepping to the cover of the shrubs. The Face Man followed him, and together they stared out through the foliage at the bizarre scene taking place at the side of the nearby pool.

Jorge, the villa's owner, was pacing before the edge of the swimming pool, script in hand as he read aloud his lines to an unclothed mannequin laid out on a chaise lounge three feet away from him. He cut a strange figure with his spindly legs and arms emanating from a torso swollen by too many multicourse meals and the consumption of locally brewed *cerveza*. Rather than a likely romantic hero, he looked more like an anthropomorphic spider circling some prey that had fallen into the sticky webwork of the chaise lounge.

"You love me, I know it, Loni," Jorge boldly addressed the mannequin, sucking in his gut and adding swagger to his step. "I am El Toro, the bull, and I long to crush you in my great arms and smother you with the ardor of my affection."

From their cover the Face Man elbowed Murdock gently and whispered, "More likely he'd smother her with the girth of his midriff."

Murdock blinked away imaginary tears and sniffed lightly as he sobbed, "You must excuse me, I can't help it. Love scenes just do this to me . . ."

"I wish I had a violin," Peck said. "Here comes the good part."

Jorge closed in on the object of his attentions, then awkwardly dropped to one knee and leaned over the mannequin, drawing his face toward the lifeless features of his imagined Loni. To Peck's and Murdock's surprise, Jorge raised his voice a few octaves and squeaked in a ridiculous falsetto meant to be the romantic cooing of Loni Anderson. "Oh, El Toro. I must have you, now. Consume me with your passion and we will light up the night with our love."

Carried away with his performance, Jorge lowered himself on top of the mannequin and began making sounds meant for the intimacy of one's bedroom.

"I thought *Boots and Bikinis* was rated PG," Murdock murmured.

"We're spicing it up for the international market," the Face Man said. "Come on, let's let these two lovebirds be alone. We've still got a lot to do."

Circling around the grounds, the two men made their way to the guest bungalows where they had been staying. After showering and changing, they helped themselves to cold beers and roasted nuts on the patio as they contemplated their next move.

"They were taken prisoner, no doubt about it," Peck said. "If they've got that whole goon squad guarding them, we're going to have our hands full trying to spring 'em."

"We'll just have to fight fire with fire, right?" Murdock said. "And here comes the man who's gonna help us."

As Miguel Perez made his way up the walk to the patio, the Face Man asked Murdock, "Fire with fire? I don't get it."

"Valdez has an army behind him, right? . . ."

"Oh, I see. That's a pretty tall order." Peck finished his beer and got up from his chair as Miguel joined them. "Well, here goes nothin' . . ."

"I just came by to see how the filming with the plane went today," Perez said, shaking Peck's hand.

"Perfecto," the Face Man said. "Matter of fact, we got it down in the first take. Put us way ahead of schedule. What we'd like to do now, if you can help swing it, is push up things and try to get in some of that footage with the Mexican Army scouring the hills.''

Perez had just eased himself into one of the chairs. He eyed Peck incredulously. "The Mexican Army?"

Peck let his good mood darken. He shook his head impatiently and planted his hands on his hips as he stared down at the film commissioner. "Yeah, the Mexican Army. What's the big deal, chickie?"

Perez had brought along his copy of the *Boots and Bikinis* screenplay. Flipping through it, he said, "But, in this script I read . . . there is nothing in here about the Army. Señor, this would take some time and doing."

"Oh, boy," Murdock groaned in the background. "We is dead meat once Andre hears about this. Cold cuts . . ."

The Face Man turned his back to Perez and walked off to the edge of the patio, as if trying to bring his rage under control. His eyes met with Murdock's and both men winked, then Peck went back to lay out his trump card. "Look, Miguel, you want it straight? I'll give it to you straight. I'm real, real disappointed with this Film Commission. I've seen the ads you guys are always running in the trades back in Hollywood . . . 'Come to Mexico,' 'Film in Splendor,' 'Make Pals with the Peso' . . . all that *bueno*, *mi compadres* junk. We bit at it and decided to give you folks a chance, ride some big money on you. But since I got down here, Mike, I've been getting nothing but complaints and arguments. I gotta pull teeth to get anything around here!"

"But, señor . . ."

"Please, Mike, give it a rest, okay?" the Face Man yelled. "I've had it. No sixteen-million-dollar transfusion for the local economy, hombre. We're outta here!"

"Wait, wait, please," Miguel pleaded, bounding out of

his seat. "Let us not do anything so hasty. Give me a chance to make some calls. Perhaps something can be arranged. . . ."

"Perhaps?" the Face Man said. "Perhaps? Perhaps is like kissing your sister."

Perez frowned, confused. "I beg your pardon? I do not understand that saying."

"Never mind. Okay, I'll give you one last chance. Grab the horn and give it your best shot. If you can get me some decent military clout to slap on celluloid, we might get through this fiasco yet. . . ."

THIRTY

Manny Cortez, B.A., and Amy were all huddled around the ravaged form of Al Massey when Hannibal was escorted back to the shell and unhandcuffed before being shoved inside.

"He doesn't look so good," Hannibal said, coming over and noticing the clammy sweat that had beaded up on the reporter's face. "How is he?"

"Bad." Amy dabbed at Massey's brow with the sleeve of her blouse. "He's got a fever. He could be bleeding inside."

"Whatever's wrong with him, he's going to need medical help, and soon," Manny said. "I wouldn't count on Valdez to provide it, either."

"I've got that feeling, too," Hannibal said, checking Massey's pulse while the injured man drifted in and out of consciousness, his breath coming in irregular spasms. "Let's try to keep his forehead dry or he's gonna drown in his own sweat."

Amy reached for her purse and shook its contents out onto the ground. As she snatched up a packet of Kleenex and placed a few of the tissues over Massey's brow,

Hannibal glanced down at the cosmetics Amy had scattered at his feet.

"Is that a tweezer?" he asked.

"What?"

"That tweezer," Hannibal said, pointing at the pronged instrument. "Let me have that, along with the mascara and your makeup kit."

"Whatever for?" Amy asked. "This is no time for—"

"Just do it, would you, Miss Allen?" Hannibal asked, his patience straining. "Trust me."

As Amy reluctantly gathered up the cosmetics and handed them to Hannibal, B.A. smirked at his cohort. "Comin' out of the closet, man?"

"Comin' from some dude who wears rings in his ears and more necklaces than the Queen of England, that's pretty funny, B.A.," Hannibal cracked back.

As Hannibal retreated to the other side of the cell and hunched over to begin making himself over, the others continued to do what they could to help Massey. The only provisions they'd been provided with had been a gourd filled with tepid water and a dust-covered loaf of stale bread. As Amy held Massey's head, Manny gently poured a small amount of the liquid over Massey's parched lips. The reporter's mouth quivered, and he managed to get down a few swallows.

"H . . . h . . . hot," he murmured weakly.

"Shhhhh, just rest, Al," Amy told him. "We're going to get through this somehow. Save up your strength."

The guards in charge of the area were preoccupied with the captured villagers in another one of the cells, who were carrying on loudly about the way they were being treated. Left unwatched, B.A. paced around the cell, testing the bars and lashings in hopes of finding a weak link he could apply his brute strength against. "Man, this is built solid," he complained. "Might as well be made outta steel."

"When all else fails," Hannibal mumbled across the way, "try shrewdness." Turning around to face B.A., Hannibal revealed himself to be transformed into a moustachioed bandito. The makeup was far from subtle, but Hannibal was out for only short-term effect, not an Oscar.

"Who you think you're gonna fool with that getup, Hannibal?" B.A. asked.

"Not the Film Commission, I'll clue you that much." Hannibal came over to B.A., then slumped down before the burly mechanic. "Okay, let's do this in one take. You lured me in here and just put a knuckle sandwich in my breadbasket, got it?"

"I think I can handle that."

"What should we do?" Amy asked.

Hannibal looked over at her and Manny. "Play it by ear. If they only send one guy in, stay outta the way and let B.A. do his thing."

With the stage set, Hannibal nodded for the performance to begin. B.A. threw a slow-motion punch into Hannibal's midriff. Hannibal folded under the supposed impact, letting out a convincing groan as he crumpled to the dirt and lay down for the ten count. The groan was loud enough to draw the attention of two guards standing at the edge of the nearest shrubs. They looked at each other, then one of the Mexicans decided to investigate while the other went to lend a hand to his comrades dealing with the rowdy villagers. The guard approaching the A-Team's cell unslung his rifle and stared suspiciously at the inert body lying at B.A.'s feet.

"*Qué pasa?*" the sentry called out.

Hannibal stirred slightly, offering a brief enough glimpse of his face to sustain the illusion that he was one of Valdez's men who'd made the mistake of going into the cell.

"*Qué te paso?!*" the sentry shouted at Hannibal with increasing agitation.

"I just punched his lights out, that's all," B.A. boasted to the guard. "Why don't you come in and see how many rounds you can last with me, sucker?"

The guard wasn't bilingual, but from the tone of B.A.'s voice and the display of the black man's middle finger, he was able to get the message. Unleashing a torrent of expletives in his native tongue, the Mexican kept his rifle trained on B.A. while he used his free hand to unlock the cell door. "*Pendejo!*" he growled at Hannibal, gesturing for him to get up and out of the cell. "*Stupido!*"

Hannibal rose slowly to his knees and inched toward the cell door, keeping his face pointed to the ground, as if ashamed at his dereliction of duty. Once he was within striking distance of the guard, however, he sprang forward with the force of an uncoiled spring. In one fluid motion, he grabbed hold of the sentry's rifle and jerked it forward with so much force that the guard stumbled headlong into the cell, where B.A. was ready with a right cross that sent him sprawling to the ground. He wouldn't be getting up for a while.

"Good show, B.A.," Hannibal congratulated his friend.

"I'd like to plant one of them into Valdez's kisser by the time we're through here," B.A. said, readjusting the rings on his fingers.

"For now let's just worry about getting away in one piece," Hannibal said. As he dragged the limp sentry off to one side and took up the fallen rifle, B.A. helped

Manny and Amy lift Al Massey and secure a strong enough grip on the wounded reporter that they could carry him with the least resistance.

With Hannibal leading the way, the prisoners made their way out of the cell and down the row of shrubs keeping them out of the view of the other guards. Fifty yards away they came upon a wide clearing filled with parked vehicles, all of them empty and untended. Threading their way through the maze of jeeps and half-tracks, the group finally came upon a medium-sized truck with a canvas shell over the rear bed. Amy and Manny climbed up into the shell, then dragged Massey in with them. Hannibal and B.A. stole their way to the front cab and got inside. As B.A. fumbled with the wiring, trying to start the engine without a key, Hannibal kept his eyes open for trouble. His finger was on the trigger of the automatic rifle in case he found it.

"Ready whenever you are," Hannibal told B.A.

"I'm workin' on it, man!" B.A. snarled, fidgeting beneath the dashboard. He finally crossed the right wires and the engine turned over dully a few times, then died. "Come on, mamma . . ."

At the same time the engine was sputtering, the guard B.A. had kayoed in the cell was coming to and letting the world know about it. His cry of alarm spread quickly, and soon a handful of armed soldiers were rushing to the area where the trucks were parked. Fortunately, there were so many vehicles cluttering the area that the sentries had trouble placing the one that carried the escaped prisoners.

As B.A. succeeded in revving the truck's engine, Hannibal looked down at the floor of the cab and exclaimed, "Oh, boy! More pineapples! How nice they're in season!" He plucked up one of the grenades and slipped a finger through the ring while B.A. found first gear and drove the truck forward, steering around the jeeps surrounding it.

"Better do something quick, Hannibal," B.A. said once he'd gotten the truck clear and was heading down the dirt road leading to potential freedom. A dozen armed guerrillas had converged on the road and were drawing bead on the truck with weapons ranging from automatic pistols to a shoulder-held bazooka.

Hannibal leaned out his window and fired a quick round of fire from his rifle, then pulled the pin on the grenade and hurled it forward, scattering the men making up the human roadblock. Just before the grenade went off, Hannibal pulled his head back inside the cab and shouted through the rear window to Manny and Amy, "Hold onto Massey, 'cause we're apt to hit a few bumps . . ."

A resounding explosion took a huge bite out of the roadway and sprayed the guards with shrapnel and flying clods of dirt. B.A. barreled the truck through the smoke, clearing the gouged earth and passing through the main gateway of the military outpost. Valdez and Colonel Flores caught up with their men, livid with rage at the escape in progress. Pointing at the retreating truck, Valdez screamed, "Shoot! Shoot! Kill them!"

A handful of the guerrillas followed orders and sent an ineffective spray of gunfire in the direction of the truck, while others began piling into other vehicles to take up the chase. Valdez and Flores climbed into one of the jeeps and braced themselves as the driver spun the rear tires against loose gravel before finding solid ground and making the speedometer rise as fast as the rebel leaders' tempers.

"I want them executed!" Flores roared. "I'll have their heads on poles for this, next to the heads of the men who let them escape!"

Out on open terrain, B.A. veered the truck around sharp bends while keeping the accelerator pressed as close to the floor as he could manage. Hannibal emptied the box of grenades out the side window, one at a time, in hopes of making the way behind them less easy to travel. Neither measure produced their intended results, however, and less than two miles away from the compound, B.A. was already spotting the outlines of tenacious jeeps gaining ground through the dusty view in his rearview mirror. They were a long way from Acapulco.

Hannibal saw them, too. "They're closing! Move it, B.A.!"

B.A. kept his foot to the floorboard but shook his head miserably. "They got us, man!"

"Hey, come on, B.A.," Hannibal chided, tossing out his last grenade. "No time for a bad attitude here . . ."

"Can't help it, man," B.A. said, pointing to the dashboard. "We're almost outta gas!"

"Out of gas?" Hannibal couldn't believe it. "Why'd you pick a truck with no gas?"

" 'Cause I liked the paint job!" B.A. yelled back. "How was I supposed to know? Man, we were on the run!"

"We still are, my friend," Hannibal said. "Let's just—"

"Whoah!" B.A. interjected. "Listen, Hannibal!"

The explosion of the last grenade boomed through the air, then Hannibal heard what B.A. had picked out moments before . . . the purring of rotors overhead.

"A chopper?" Hannibal said, daring to hope. "There weren't any choppers back at the fort, were there?"

"Not that I saw," B.A. replied.

The shadow of a helicopter swept across the road before

them, and Hannibal risked sticking his head out the window for a better look.

"It's Murdock!" he called out. "Hang the first right you can. It looks like he's gonna put down over by that grove of palm trees. . . ."

The road ran straight and unbroken, so B.A. had to keep his eyes open for a stretch of shoulder he could ram the truck over without tipping or bounding too wildly. He finally spotted a semiclearing and veered through it, edging up a mild slope that leveled off to the patch of flatland where Murdock was in the process of landing the helicopter. The chopper had the insignia of the Mexican Army emblazoned on its side, and the airship's hold seemed large enough to carry a few A-Teams.

Hannibal hopped out of the truck just as the Face Man was dropping from the helicopter and hunching over as he moved clear of the rooftop propeller.

"Hey, great, Face," Hannibal said, slapping Peck on the back. "You brought the cavalry! Where's the rest of the guys?"

"Sorry, Hannibal, I couldn't get the whole Army," the Face Man shouted above the roar of the rotors. "I barely managed to wrangle this camera ship here. We're loaded with AR-15s for props, too . . ."

"Lotta good guns are going to do us with nobody to use 'em," Hannibal said, his hopes fading. "We've got a whole guerrilla band chompin' at our tails . . ."

"Hey, hey, I just said we couldn't get the *Army*," the Face Man said. With a sweep of his arm, he motioned to the surrounding palms. "Voilà!"

Like bugs creeping out of the woodwork, men began to appear between the towering palms, making their way up the hillside and across the clearing toward the truck and helicopter. Hannibal flinched with a flash of fear until he began to recognize some of the faces of the men, who wore street clothes instead of military uniforms.

"We stopped by San Rio Blanco to see if you'd turned up. They insisted on helping us come look for you."

"Well, well, well." Hannibal beamed, watching on as the men of San Rio Blanco nodded quick greetings on their way to the helicopter, where the Face Man and Murdock began handing out the weapons that had been stored in the hold.

B.A. got out of the truck and came over to Hannibal's side, punching him playfully on the shoulder as he said, "Yeah, yeah, Hannibal, you just love it when a plan comes together."

THIRTY-ONE

"Once we crush these vermin under our heels, we will have no further problems," Valdez gloated to Colonel Flores as the two men rode at the head of the guerrilla force, dodging the pothole made by the last grenade Hannibal had thrown their way. A dozen other jeeps brought up the rear, carrying another fifty men.

"If we would have gotten rid of that reporter at the start, we would not be having these problems in the first place," Flores reminded Valdez. "It was your idea that we keep him alive and try to get a ransom for him. . . ."

"No matter," Valdez said, pointing to where tracks in the dirt betrayed the detour B.A. had taken in hopes of evading the A-Team's pursuers. "We will end things now, once and for all."

The lead jeep waited for the other vehicles to catch up, then the assembled force poured up the hillside leading to the palm grove. Less than halfway up, the foliage came alive with activity, exploding with raucous gunfire. Bullets ripped through the earth around the advancing jeeps, then leapt up at the vehicles themselves. Caught by surprise, the drivers overreacted. Some slammed on brakes and skidded wildly to one side, colliding with those jeeps whose riders had tried to steer away from the ambush. In the resultant chain reaction, the entire fleet of jeeps was rendered immobile. The soldiers leapt out and scrambled frantically for cover, but the fusillade from the brush was relentless, and no place seemed safe from the ambushers' aim.

"Okay, we've got 'em corralled," Face Man said, staring down the slope at the skirmish. "Now all we gotta do is make sure they all get properly branded. No strays, gentlemen."

"We'll keep an eye on things from the air," Hannibal said before ducking over and running back to the helicopter. Murdock was already behind the controls, and once Hannibal boarded, the chopper pulled up and away.

"That means we take the low road," Peck said, running alongside B.A. and Amy toward the truck. Al Massey had already been taken out of the back, and he waved to them from the shade of a nearby palm, where he was being guarded by several villagers.

"Spit in V-Valdez's eye for m-me," he called out weakly, managing a smile.

As he got in behind the wheel and started up the engine, B.A. said, "I just hope we don't have to chase down anybody too far, 'cause our gas tank's touchin' the big E, and that don't stand for excellent. . . ."

Sitting next to B.A., the Face Man reached over and threw a switch beneath the dashboard. "I'm surprised at you, B.A.," he said casually as he slammed a cartridge into his automatic rifle. "I would have thought you'd know this monster has a reserve tank. We're golden."

"How about that," B.A. muttered. "Ya learn somethin' new every day." He looked out the back window of the cab and saw Amy taking up her position toward the rear of the truck, a rifle clutched in her hands as if she knew how to use it. She glanced at him over her shoulder and gave him the okay sign. B.A. shifted into first and drove off, circling around the battle below. Whenever they spotted some of the enemy attempting to retreat, they bore down and sent a volley of lead to escort them back to the action.

The ambush had been well executed, and it was only a matter of minutes before the trapped guerrillas realized the futility of their position. One by one they began tossing down their weapons and throwing up their hands, and finally the only gunfire was coming from the proud defenders of San Rio Blanco. They emerged from cover, exultant at their part in the capture. As the citizens formed a human circle around their oppressors, they let forth a chorus of cheers.

In the commotion two furtive figures stole through the labyrinth of crumpled jeeps until they came across one that was still in running condition. After pausing to make certain that they hadn't been spotted, Malavida Valdez and Colonel Flores bounded into the vehicle. Before anyone could stop them, the two desperadoes were speeding down the hill toward the main road, almost running over the three men of the village who stood in their way.

Up in the helicopter Hannibal was quick to pick up the course of the runaway jeep.

"What's this?" he said to himself. He snapped his fingers to get Murdock's attention, then pointed down at the terrain. "Couple of guests look like they're leaving before the bash is over. Let's go have a word with 'em, shall we?''

"My pleasure." Murdock promptly banked the chopper and swept down through the palms to take up pursuit of the jeep. Securing himself in the seat, Hannibal leaned out the chopper enough to get off a clear shot. He perforated the jeep's hood, damaging enough of the engine to halt its forward progress. Behind the wheel Valdez tried to roll the vehicle to cover, but the moment he left the road, he discovered one of the craters formed by a recently tossed grenade. The jeep pitched sharply down into the hole, throwing its riders against the windshield and then out onto the ground. Murdock circled around so that Hannibal could fire off another round and convince the enemy leaders that surrender was in their best interests. By the time Murdock had brought the chopper back down in the nearest clearing, villagers had apprehended Flores and Valdez and led them back to the other prisoners.

"Boy, it sure is a shame we *didn't* have cameras for this one," Hannibal reflected as he and Murdock jogged over to join their fellow members of the A-Team. "Mr. Perez would have been most impressed."

"Hell, if they'd put this kind of footage all the way through *Boots and Bikinis*, I might even learn to like that movie. . . ." Murdock said.

Colonel Flores and Malavida Valdez might have conceded the moment, but neither of them seemed defeated when they were confronted by the A-Team moments later.

"You better have one hell of an apology ready," Hannibal told the two men.

"Pah!" Valdez said, spitting in the dirt. "You have a

few of us now, but soon the rest of our force will be here, and it is us who will have the upper hand.''

"I wouldn't count on it, pal,'' Hannibal drawled lazily. ''I've dealt with enough rat packs like yours to know that once the leaders are under wraps, everyone else runs like hell to make sure the same thing doesn't happen to them. Why, right about now, I figure your men are probably running off in ten different directions, none of them this way.''

Manny Cortez came over to Hannibal's side, holding an automatic rifle. "You have been a great help to us,'' he said, ''but now we feel strong enough to stand on our own two feet. We will see that these people are dealt with justly for what they've done.''

"Sounds good to me,'' Hannibal said, shaking Manny's hand. ''Glad to be of service to a good cause.''

As Manny took over supervision of the operation, Hannibal and Murdock went over to the truck to join B.A., the Face Man, and Amy.

"Well done, ladies and gentlemen,'' Hannibal told them.

Just then two of the stronger villagers made their way down the hill, carrying Al Massey on a makeshift stretcher between them. One of them told Murdock, ''If we load him into the helicopter, we can show you where to fly him for treatment in Acapulco.''

Murdock looked over at Hannibal, who nodded his approval of the plan.

Before he was led away, Massey struggled slightly to lift his head and sputter, ''I . . . th-thank you.''

"Just make sure you're healed before you start grabbing for headlines,'' Hannibal advised him.

Massey nodded and eased back on the stretcher. Amy

accompanied him aways, whispering encouragement in his ear, then backtracked to rejoin the A-Team. "You did it!" she exclaimed gratefully. "You saved him. I don't know how to thank you . . ."

Hannibal reached to his pocket, withdrawing a wrapped cigar. As he opened the wrapper and tapped it out, he looked at Amy and grinned. "We'll send you a bill. . . ."